LOVE PUCKED

Cover Design by Emily Wittig Designs

Editing by Happily Editing Anns

www.authoremilysilver.com

LOVE PUCKED

A Toronto Rosebuds Novel

EMILY SILVER

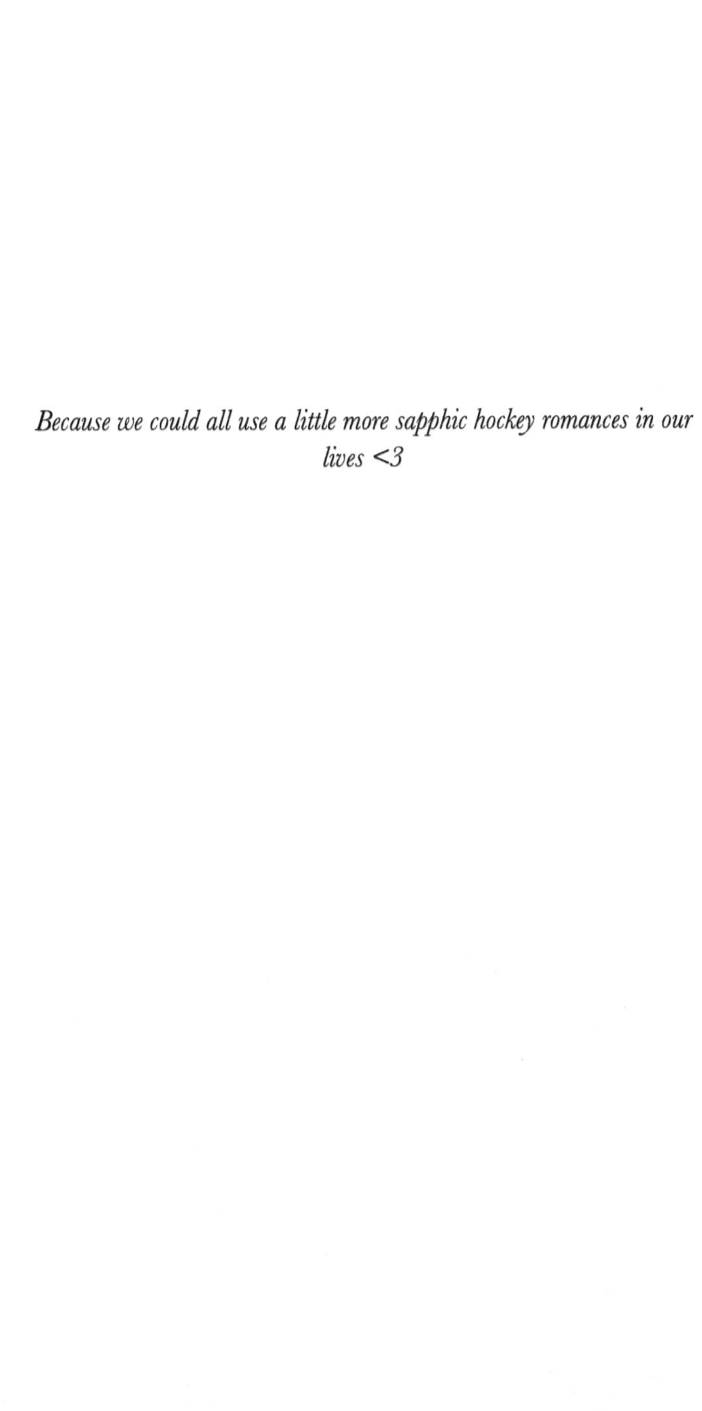

Because we could all use a little more sapphic hockey romances in our lives <3

Chapter One

DELANEY

This is it. The moment I've been working toward for the last two years.

A head coaching position.

Ever since I quit playing, it's what I've wanted.

No.

What I've dreamed of.

Coaching the next generation of female hockey players?

It's all I want.

Sitting in a bland office building in the middle of Toronto, I try not to let my nerves get the best of me. After working my way up in the coaching world the last few years, it's not cocky to say I know I'm good. Now, with the women's professional league expanding to Toronto, it's everything I've dreamed of.

Being a head coach.

"Ms. Charles?"

A younger woman calls my name and I stand, smoothing the front of my black dress pants.

I've put everything into my appearance today.

A brand-new red blouse to project confidence. A black blazer. Pressed pants and a sensible pair of heels. My dark brown bob sleek and newly trimmed.

I'm ready to nail this interview.

The woman leads me to an open conference room that overlooks the small park behind it. Three older men sit on the other side of the table. I recognize them as the owner, the president, and the general manager.

Also known as the three people tasked with hiring the next coach of the Toronto Rosebuds.

"Ms. Charles. Thank you for taking the time to meet us today."

"It's my pleasure." I shake their proffered hands before taking my seat.

No nerves, Delaney. You're a badass and deserve to be here.

"Ms. Charles, can we get you anything before we get started?" the woman who led me in here asks.

"No, thank you."

She nods and backs her way out of the room, leaving me with these three imposing men.

"Why do you want to coach in Toronto, Ms. Charles?" the owner asks. "Why this team? Why not, say, Minneapolis?"

I straighten my spine. I have prepared for every question they could have fired at me. Even if it's an easy one to start with.

"Please, call me Delaney. I want to coach here because I want to get in at the ground level and coach a team from the very start. Toronto has a history of being a proud sports city, and I want to be a part of that. I want to coach a team that this city wants to get behind and women that are strong players. With a smaller league, it's harder to accomplish, but I want to establish Toronto as the team to beat."

Their heads nod in agreement. Being that there are now only six teams in the women's league, it's hard to make a name for yourself.

"And how do you see yourself leading the Rosebuds?" This coming from the president.

I still hate that team name. The Rosebuds. Could they have come up with anything less hockey than the Rosebuds?

I won't earn any favors by telling them that.

"I want to lead by example. Having played hockey before, I know what it takes to win. What it takes to win with a head coach that believes in you and the team. I've had my fair sure of good and bad coaches, and it's made me realize how I want to lead. With kindness and compassion, but at the same time, a firm hand to make sure we're the best we can be."

Questions are fired at me left and right, and I answer them with ease.

I've been preparing for this interview ever since I watched the announcement that they were expanding the women's league. You can't have hockey without having a team in Toronto. It's sacrilegious. The logistics of getting a team here took too long when the new league was founded.

When the women's league was started, the city was in the process of building a new rink for the men's team. With that glass monstrosity complete, the women will move into the men's old rink.

Granted, it got its own shiny upgrade, but not as fancy as the men's team.

Something I'm used to.

But it doesn't matter. Because all I want to do is lead Toronto's first ever women's hockey team.

"You will hear from us soon, Delaney. Thank you for

taking the time to come in today." It's hard to get a read on them, but I catch the glances they exchange.

They look positive. I mean, it's not saying much, because I don't think they'd give much away. But it plants a seed of hope inside me.

"Thank you. It would be an honor to be Toronto's first head coach."

I shake their hands and leave the office building. The warm, Toronto air fills my lungs as I step outside. The sun shines bright as I turn on the sidewalk and pull out my phone and dial the one person who might be more excited than I am.

"Hey, baby. How'd it go?"

Mom's chipper voice makes me happy. "It went really well. I think I might have a shot."

She scoffs. "If they have any sense, they would have hired you on the spot. You took Vermont's team to the championship within two years. And won!"

"I know."

I listen as she rattles off everything I've done so far in my career. When I started as an assistant coach with Vermont University a few years back, the team was terrible. But after a few years, things started to improve. After their old coach retired, I took over, and within two years, we won the championship.

I love working with college athletes, shaping them into the players they are, but when this opportunity landed in my lap, I couldn't say no.

"Do you know who else is in the running?" she asks.

"No idea."

"Any word on which players they're getting?"

"Not yet."

With the league expanding, they're transferring players

around and bringing up people from the minor leagues. Putting everyone on equal ground.

"Well, they will be lucky to have you."

"Thanks, Mom. But let's not count on it just yet."

"I can picture it now. My daughter. The head coach of the Rosebuds." She ignores me, like any mother who believes in her child does. "Now, if only you can find a nice man to settle down with."

"Right. Listen, I have to go. Love you, Mom."

"Love you too, baby. Keep me posted."

"I will."

I swallow down the bile in my throat. It's something that I've never had the courage to tell my mom—that I'm not into men, but women.

Anytime I would get close, something would happen that would stop me from confessing who I really love to her. Even at the ripe age of thirty-five, I'm still scared.

I know I shouldn't be, but I am. Besides, it's not like I'm dating anyone. It's not a pressing issue. I'll cross that bridge when I get there.

If ever...

Chapter Two

LYDIA

"**I**s this the last box?" Troy whines, dropping another box onto the dining room table. "I don't know how many more trips for shoes I can manage."

"Stop it." I swat at him and check the side of the box. "This isn't even shoes."

"Then what is it? It's fucking heavy."

"Pots and pans."

"Do you even cook that much?" he gripes, wiping the sweat from his brow.

I can't blame him. It's a warm day in Toronto, and with moving all my boxes and furniture, it's not exactly cool inside.

"Yes. I'll have you know I'm very good at it."

"She's the only one of our kids that can somehow manage not to burn water," Derek states, setting his box down on the kitchen counter.

"I resent that," Troy says. "I'm good at cooking."

"Then why am I the chef in the house?" Angie quirks her brow at him, starting to unpack one of the boxes.

Seeing as how my sister-in-law is pregnant, Troy won't

let her lift a finger to help. Unpacking boxes is about all she can do.

"I really don't like when you two gang up on me," he complains.

My stepdad claps him on the shoulder. "Then come help me with Lyd's mattress and we'll be done."

"Fucking finally."

"It hasn't been that bad!" I shout after them.

Since I'll need my car in Toronto, I figured it would be easier to pack up and move myself by pulling a trailer filled with my belongings. My mom wouldn't let me do it alone, so my family met me here to help. Sure, I could have hired movers, but it's one thing I don't like giving up control over.

"C'mon. Let's start unpacking the kitchen." Angie taps away on her phone. "I'm ordering the pizza and we'll need this place ready when it gets here."

"Works for me."

The place I found is small. Not that the women's professional hockey league brings in the big bucks, but as one of the stars, I make a good salary. One I still don't want to blow entirely on a house when I don't know where I'll be in a few years' time. Until then, apartment living is the way to go.

At least this place has a bedroom and is an upgrade from my studio in Boston. The living room is small with room for only one couch, but there's a nice outdoor patio. It's the one thing I love.

Getting to be outside in the city makes the tiny apartment feel less cramped.

"Are you excited to be here?" Angie asks, tucking a lock of long brown hair behind her ear.

I waggle my head back and forth. "Yeah, but I'm

nervous. It's been a while since I moved, so it's like that first day of school feeling."

"Wondering if all the kids are going to like you?" Angie asks.

"Why wouldn't they like you?" Mom asks, handing over a stack of plates. "You were the highest scoring player in the league last year. Toronto clearly wanted you, otherwise they wouldn't have shelled out the big bucks to get you."

That pulls a smile to my face. "I don't know if that will still be the case this year. There are a lot of talented people on the Rosebuds."

With restructuring the league to expand to ten teams instead of six, players from all the teams were moved around. There were logistic issues getting the team started in Toronto from the initiation of the league, but now, it seems, with so much talent being shifted, it's anyone's guess as to which team will come out on top.

"None as talented as you," Mom points out.

Leave it to her to be my biggest fan.

"Thanks. I'm just ready to get started."

It's that time in the offseason where I'm getting antsy. I'm working out almost every day to get in season-ready shape. I'm on the ice a few days a week, but I want to train with my new teammates.

"Will the famous Bishop walk-in still be a thing here?" Angie asks.

"Duh," I scoff. "I'll do that no matter what team I'm playing for."

It's one of the things I love about the game. The pregame walk-ins. Fashion has always been my thing—hence my brother griping about carrying my shoes up to my apartment. I love making an appearance when I come to the game. Getting free clothes to model from top designers by wearing them to the game?

I love it. I work hard for my body, so why can't I show it off?

"Good. You know I'll be jealous of everything I can't wear that you can."

I smile at her as her hand rests on her burgeoning belly. "Clothes that I will gladly send your way after my niece is born."

"As long as you hand deliver them so you can meet her."

"I can't wait to spoil her. You'll start to get sick of me being there visiting."

"Start to?" my brother huffs out, backing his way through the front door. "Who says we're not already sick of you?"

"Troy," they all say in unison.

"Kidding." He drops the mattress against the wall, shaking his arms out. "When is lunch getting here? I'm starving."

"Should be here soon," Angie tells him, walking over to give him a kiss.

The two of them are still disgustingly in love all these years later.

"How's it going in here?" Derek asks, grabbing a glass that sits on the counter to fill it with water.

"Well, kitchen is almost done," Mom starts, "so I guess we'll need to get going on the living room and bedroom."

"I can do my room," I tell her. "Bed frame is already set up, so it shouldn't be hard."

"You know we're here for a few days to help, right?" Derek asks. "We don't mind helping. Even your brother doesn't."

"Really?" I laugh.

"He likes giving you shit."

I grab the scissors and rip open another box. "Don't you have practice starting soon?"

Derek shakes his head. "Not as important as getting you settled. My coaches can handle it while I'm gone."

He's been the head coach for the same high school football team since he and my mom started dating more than twenty-five years ago. Ever since he quit playing, he's been coaching.

And based on the number of state championships they've brought home, he's the best out there. He could have moved up to the college level, but he never wanted to. He liked the stability of being able to be there for his family during the offseason.

Something my real dad never did once Mom and Derek got married.

A buzzer shakes me from my thoughts.

"Thank God. I'm starving." Troy bolts to the door and buzzes in whoever is on the other side.

"Did you even stop to check and make sure it was pizza?" Mom asks. "What if it was a serial killer?"

We all laugh.

"Sutton, do you really think a serial killer would buzz themselves in?" Derek asks.

"Nothing wrong with making sure she's safe. Do you—"

"Have my pepper spray? Yes, in my purse," I interrupt. "Good."

Garlic and marinara aromas permeate the small space. It takes everything in me not to point out to my mom that it wasn't a serial killer.

Troy grabs the pizzas and passes them to Derek before fishing out some money for a tip. "Thanks."

Plates, drinks, and pizza are passed around as we settle

around the small kitchen table. It only has seating for four. Nothing else would fit in the space. I stand, letting everyone else sit since they're helping me.

I tear off the tip of the pizza, hungrier than I thought. The feta, olive oil, and roasted red peppers are just what I needed today. Nothing like spending the morning moving to work up an appetite.

"Do you know any of your new teammates yet?" Angie asks.

I shrug a shoulder. "I've played against most of them, so hopefully that'll help with the team gelling."

"It's always hard with new teammates," Derek says. "Be the amazing person I know you are, and it'll be an easy transition."

I smile at him. "Thanks."

In moments like this, I know why Derek still coaches. He could have retired years ago, but he loves what he does. He's amazing at it. I think it's why I started playing hockey to begin with. He took us to the rink in the mornings when we were little to help us learn to skate. It was what we did together—Derek, Troy, and me.

I loved it.

"Think you'll win a championship?" Troy elbows me in the side, grabbing another slice of pizza.

"I have to. You can't be the only one to win one."

"Two," he corrects. "Don't forget, it's two now."

"I'm surprised your ego can fit in this apartment." Angie rolls her eyes at her husband.

"What?" He looks at her. "She brings it out in me."

I shrug. "I can't help it if I'm the better hockey player."

"And here I thought the two of them would have put this childish nonsense behind them when they hit adulthood." Derek sighs.

"I don't think that will ever happen," Mom says.

"Never," we answer together.

"I'm rethinking this having multiple children now." Angie laughs.

"You'll love them, Angie, even when they're bickering," Mom states before looking at both of us. "Well, most days."

"I resent that."

"Hey!"

We both guffaw.

"You started it," I tell Troy.

"You did."

"Okay," Derek interrupts us. "Why don't we finish setting up the furniture and then we can leave you to unpack your room, Lyd?"

"Works for me."

I love that they all came to help, but I am ready to open a bottle of wine, blast some music, and get my room sorted. Not matter where I am, my room is what always feels like home.

Now? Toronto is home.

Chapter Three

LYDIA

It's not my first day at the rink, but it's my first time here for an official team event. An important one.

Today is the day that the Toronto Rosebuds are announcing their new head coach.

I'm anxious to see who they picked. There are a lot of talented coaches out there. The front-runner is the assistant coach from Detroit's NHL team.

I watched footage of him behind the bench. He's good. He'd be a great coach to play for. My guess is it'll be him.

Heading into the locker room, I'm excited to see the Rosebuds logo hanging on the back wall. The Toronto skyline is lit up behind it.

Gray carpet with a single rosebud is stretched across the floor. Wooden lockers sit in the space, each with a leather cushion embossed with a rosebud. Our names hang on the lockers in number order.

Smiling, I know exactly where to find mine.

A few women are already here, chatting in the corners. I find number twenty-two, and the two women on either side of me are already there.

"Well, if it isn't *the* Lydia Bishop," the woman I recognize as Parker White says by way of greeting. "Damn if I'm not excited to play with you."

I take her hand and shake it. It's a firm grip, like mine.

Something I can chalk up to Derek—my real dad was never around long enough to teach me about the importance of a firm handshake.

"If it isn't *the* Parker White," I fire back at her, smiling. "Minneapolis's best goaltender."

"I'm surprised they let you go," the woman on my other side says. "I'd have locked you in."

I turn to face her and stick out my hand for her to shake. "Nice to officially meet you, Skylar."

"You too."

Skylar Thorson is a stunner. If she were single, I'd want to date her. But last I heard, she's been in a long-term relationship with a college boyfriend. Long brown hair that flows past her shoulders is curled, and her face is perfectly made up. Her brown eyes are sparkling.

In a form-fitting black dress and heels, you would never guess she's a hockey player. More like a model plucked from a runway during fashion week.

"I guess we'll be locker buddies this season," Parker says.

Parker is about as different from Skylar as you can get. In a pair of barrel jeans and a Rosebuds polo, she has a harder look about her. Her brown hair is cut short just below her ears and her hazel eyes are searching the locker room. For what, I don't know.

"Did you all think we'd end up here?" I ask, taking my seat between them. As far as my outfit, I'm somewhere in the middle of these two women.

I wanted to look nice, but am still in the process of sorting through all of my clothes. In a pair of black leather pants and a pink blouse, I opted to wear heels to feel more confident today.

Nothing like a group of women all being thrown into the same room for the first time to feel like I'm back in high school again.

I left my makeup light, wanting my blue eyes to shine today as I meet my new teammates.

"Honestly? You never know where any of us are going to end up at any point," Skylar says.

Parker whistles. "Ain't that the truth."

"Did you think you'd stay in Minneapolis?"

She nods. "I did. I guess no one was safe from restructuring."

"It'll be fun, though, to have more teams to play against."

"Aren't you the optimist?" Skylar says, resting one hand on the top shelf of her locker and leaning close. "Are you the type that thinks we'll win every game?"

I beam up at her. "When I'm on the ice? Hell, yeah."

"Damn straight." Parker holds out her fist for me to bump. "We're going to be the team to beat this year."

"We've got a good group of people here," Skylar says.

I nod. "I'm excited for it."

"Now if we can see who our coach is," Parker states. "Do you really think it'll be Detroit's guy?"

"He's good," Skylar tells us. "Took Detroit far last year. If we don't get him, I'm sure Carolina or Miami will."

I laugh. "It's still weird to me that they expanded the league into two of the warmest states out there."

Skylar shakes her head. "I wouldn't mind being traded there. I do not handle the cold well."

"We'll make sure to get you a good winter coat then," Parker tells her.

Another one of my new teammates comes up to us.

"Hey, ladies. Sorry to break up the love fest, but time to head toward the press room."

"Thanks."

Standing, I run my hands over my pants to make sure they look okay. Not that the coach is going to base her first impression on how straight my pants are.

But I want to put a good foot forward.

Skylar walks ahead of us as Parker stays by my side. "Are you dating anyone?"

I shake my head. "No. Haven't dated anyone in a while. Not for lack of trying."

"Same. No good women out there."

"The men I dated were lackluster at best and the women? They didn't understand how hard it was to be a professional hockey player. Hell, half of them didn't even realize there was a women's league."

"Ouch." Parker whistles. "That has to hurt."

"It stung. I mean, it's not like it's the first year."

The Professional Women's Hockey League was established three years ago. Having played for the national team before then, I was with Boston from the start.

"Well, between you and me then, we can focus on hockey this year."

"Sounds like a good plan to me. I want to win the cup."

"God, me too. I thought we had a shot last year in Minneapolis, but Detroit pulled the rug out from under us."

I wince. Minneapolis was winning the series, poised to steal it in four games. Out of nowhere, Detroit found their energy and ended up coming back to win the series.

If you were a Minneapolis fan, it was hard to watch. If you were a Detroit fan? You were ecstatic.

"Sorry. That had to be hard."

"You have no idea."

Having gotten to know Angie's brother, the goalie for the Black Diamonds, I know how hard they take losses. I would not want to carry that weight on my shoulders.

Filing into the press room, we take the empty seats next to Skylar. We're seated behind the rows of press and upper management. The president is chatting with the owner of the team.

I try to find anyone that looks official. Carrying themselves like a leader, like they're our coach, but I don't see anyone.

The team's logo is strewn across the banner on the backdrop behind the press table along with our main sponsors. That's another thing I have to handle before practice starts. Working with the team to figure out how my sponsorships will transfer.

The team owner gets up on the makeshift stage and taps the microphone that rests on the table. Three chairs sit behind it, with a black tablecloth draped over the table.

"Thank you, everyone, for coming to the first press conference for the newly formed Toronto Rosebuds." The owner pauses while everyone in the room claps. There's a thrill of energy that seems to float through the room. It's taken way too long to get a women's hockey team to Toronto. And even though I might not have wanted to be traded from Boston, I'm excited to be here.

"It's with great enthusiasm that I welcome Delaney Charles as our new head coach."

Wait, what? Delaney Charles? There is no way I heard him correctly. But when everyone stands and starts applauding for the woman walking into the room, my eyes don't deceive me.

There she is.

Delaney.

As in Delaney Charles, my ex-girlfriend. Star player for the women's national team who ruptured her ACL, ending her career.

She's our coach?

Fuck me.

"Are you okay?" Skylar elbows me in the side.

"Why wouldn't I be?"

"Well, you're muttering under your breath, so I wanted to check and see if you're okay or not."

"I'm fine," I tell her.

How do I tell the woman I've just met what the woman on stage means to me?

I was picked up by the national team out of college. The one person I met there that stuck with me? Delaney Charles.

She was in the prime of her career. The player every young girl aspired to be. Delaney was a phenomenal player. Her awareness on the ice wasn't something that could be taught. It was second nature to her.

God, I wanted to be her when she was a player. I settled for sleeping with her.

And now she'll be coaching me.

Seriously. How in the world did this happen?

"Good afternoon, everyone." Delaney adjusts the mic and takes her seat.

She looks exactly how I remember her and different all at the same time.

Her long, dark hair is now cut into a short, blunt bob. In a white blouse, black pants, and a blazer—affixed with a Toronto Rosebuds pin—she looks every bit of a coach.

"As Mr. Sanders said, I am Delaney Charles and it is an honor to be announced as Toronto's new head coach."

Her brown eyes gaze around the room. They go right by me, not seeing.

"It's exciting to see the PWHL expanding and growing. Not only are we now part of the league, but so are another three teams. It means good things for women in not only hockey, but sports overall."

It's hard to focus on what Delaney is saying. I still remember the last day I saw her.

It was the day of her injury. The one that ruptured her ACL and MCL. It was a nasty hit. It wasn't intentional, but the way she hit the ice? It was bad. It brought everyone to their knees.

We were playing in Finland, a proud sporting country, but that day? You could have heard a pin drop it was so quiet in the arena.

We lost the game and had to leave for home the next day. Without Delaney. It was a gut-wrenching feeling to see her left behind. I visited her in the hospital, but that was it.

I wanted to stay with her, but it's not like I could tell the team we were…what? Seeing each other?

Delaney and I were casual. No dates, but sleeping together exclusively. Not necessarily girlfriends, but it felt like it at the time. I only had eyes for her.

But being stranded in a foreign country? I hated the idea of her being left behind.

Seeing the woman in the front of the room feels like that was from a different lifetime. The Delaney I knew was fun and carefree. This person seems to be carrying the weight of the world on her shoulders.

"Thank you, Ms. Charles, for being here with us today. We are going to open it up to questions before allowing our new coach to meet with the team."

A few people clap as hands shoot into the air and Delaney's name is called out.

God. Delaney Charles.

What I wouldn't give to have this be five years ago. To see Delaney and get to have a few words with her.

Now, I'm going to have to figure out how to be around the woman that had me all twisted up all those years ago.

Chapter Four

LYDIA

"How do you feel about our new coach?" Skylar asks.

We're back in the locker room, waiting around for the press to come in to grill us about the coach announcement.

What do you think of Ms. Charles?

How do you think she'll lead the team?

Are you excited for your new coach?

I can hear all the questions now.

"I think she'll be great. She did a great job at Vermont," Parker states.

"What happened to the guy from Detroit?" I ask. "I thought he was a shoo-in for the position."

"Got an issue with Delaney?" Parker drops down into her seat, kicking her feet out and crossing them at the ankles.

"Not at all."

"You said you knew her?" Skylar asks.

"You do?" Parker pipes up. "Did you play together on the national team?"

The door to the locker room bangs open. Reporters

filter in. I recognize none of them. Having played in Boston for a few years, I got friendly with a few of them.

The ones that always gave you the soft questions after a hard loss. I liked them. They could read the room and give you the space you needed.

"How about we go out for drinks after this and I'll fill you in?"

Parker nods and Skylar's eyes sparkle. I have a feeling the three of us are going to become fast friends.

A few reporters spot the three of us and make a beeline toward us.

"Lydia Bishop. It's nice to meet you. I'm Dave Green with the *Toronto Post*. Welcome to Toronto."

"Thank you." I give him a smile as he pushes his phone closer to me to record the conversation.

"Let's dive right into it. Having come from the Boston Fury, how are you going to adjust to a new team?"

I straighten, tucking a loose lock of blonde hair behind my ear. "As it always is with a new team, there will be a learning curve. Having played against many of these women before I think will be a strength for us. We know each other's moves and that will help us in creating a team that Toronto will be proud to cheer for."

"I know everyone in town is excited that we finally have a team," he tells me.

"Toronto is synonymous with hockey, and I can't wait to be a part of it. It's about time you got a women's team."

He laughs. "Well, we're all excited for it. And even more excited that they brought in Delaney Charles as the head coach. What are your thoughts on her?"

My thoughts on Delaney Charles as head coach? I haven't been around her long enough to form that opinion.

Delaney Charles as my ex? I have a lot of thoughts on that subject. But I keep those to myself.

I clear my throat, gathering my thoughts. "I played with Delaney years ago, and she was a force to be reckoned with on the ice. I know she will bring that same passion and drive to her coaching."

"Do you think it'll be a benefit to you that you know her so well?"

I nod. "I do. I think her knowledge of the game will be an asset to the Rosebuds, and I'm looking forward to playing under her tutelage."

"Thanks, Lydia. Welcome to Toronto."

I smile back at the reporter. "Thank you. I'm excited to be here."

He moves on to the next player, leaving me alone with Parker.

"Okay, there is definitely more to this story, and I want to hear it."

I shrug a shoulder, going for casual. "We used to play together. That's it. Not much else to tell."

A smile spreads across her face. "Which means there is a story."

Great. Now I have to figure out how to get her off my back.

Until the woman in question comes into the room.

DELANEY

GOD, I'm nervous.

For the first time, I'm actually nervous. Butterflies have taken up residence in my stomach and I don't think they're ever going to leave.

I knew I was the woman for the job when I had the

interview. When I got the call? I was elated.

All I ever wanted was this, and now it's finally in my grasp.

Except for one small, minor detail.

Lydia Bishop.

My ex.

Fuck me.

I get the opportunity of a lifetime and one of the women I'm coaching is my ex?

Seriously, how does this happen?

Smoothing a hand down the front of my blazer, I make sure the Rosebuds pin is straight and step into the locker room.

A large, U-shaped space greets me. The lockers line the outside of the walls with an oversized picture of the Toronto skyline hanging above them.

This isn't my first time in here. When I got the job, this was the first place I came. It was dark and quiet. Perfect for getting acquainted with my new home away from home.

Looking around, a few members of the Rosebuds press team are here to capture this moment. Having been at the collegiate level the last few years, I spent the time since accepting the position familiarizing myself with every member of the team.

Except one.

Lydia might be one of the most talented hockey players I've ever seen. Men *or* women. She is a once in a generation talent.

The Rosebuds are lucky to have her.

I take a deep breath, steeling my nerves because I can't let myself show that she gets to me.

That's the old Delaney that fell for Lydia. The new Delaney? She has no feelings about Lydia Bishop.

Lydia Bishop who?

See? I've got this.

"Hi, everyone," I call out to the room. I don't have to wait long for them to quiet down. All eyes move to mine.

Scanning the room, I take in every single woman here. I'm quick to move over Lydia, but I don't miss the way her perfectly manicured brow rises ever so slightly.

"I know practice doesn't officially start until next week, but I wanted to thank everyone for coming in early. As you heard, I'm Delaney Charles, and I'll be your coach this season. As some of you might now, I came from Vermont, but before that, I used to play for the women's national team. I know that this is the first time a lot of you will be playing together on the same team, but you know each other from your time in the league. Others, you got called up for the first time. I'm excited for this group of women that we have and can't wait to see what we can put together on the ice."

A few nod their heads at my words. It makes it easier to know they are listening. Keeping my eyes away from the corner Lydia is standing in, I continue.

"You'll find that I'm pretty even-keeled. We'll celebrate our wins, but I don't want them going to your heads. Or our losses. I see everything, even wins, as a learning opportunity. We'll work together as a team, and that means win or lose. If we can do that, we can go far."

A few people clap and nod their heads.

"I'll see you all Monday morning for practice. I look forward to getting to know everyone better these next few weeks. I'll be in my office for the rest of the afternoon if anyone wants to stop in on their way out. I have an open-door policy, so if you ever need to talk, I'm here for you. Now, let's make this a great season."

Heading out of the locker room, I take in the concrete walls as I head back to my office past old photos of the coliseum. A few logos from sponsors are splashed here and there. It might not be the newest rink, but I'm glad there's now a women's team here.

Opening the door, I head into the sanctuary that is my office. It's one of the things I take great pride in wherever I coach.

I don't want a stark office, one that doesn't feel warm and welcoming.

When I told the owner and president this, they were all for it. Said it would make the women feel comfortable playing for me. I'm glad they were on board.

Instead of the drab white, I chose to paint the walls a light sage color to complement the berry-colored sofa. A TV sits across from the couch, making it easier to watch film, while my desk faces the window that overlooks the main street. Not a great view by any means—more concrete buildings—but it's better than my last office where I was tucked away in the basement of the arena since it was shared with the men's team.

A dry-erase board hangs next to the TV so we can work on plays as we watch them. An old jersey of mine is on the opposite side. One of the few tributes to my playing days.

"Well, well, well."

Goose bumps ripple over my skin at the sound of that voice. One I used to know so well.

Spinning on my heel, I face the woman who I left all those years ago without a word.

Lydia Bishop.

I do everything in my power to keep my eyes on hers. I don't need to see the rest of her to know how gorgeous she is. Even more so than when we first met.

"Hello."

She steps into my office and crosses her arms over her

chest. "Imagine my surprise when you walked into the room to be announced as the new head coach of the Rosebuds."

Walking backward until I find my desk, I rest my ass on the edge of it, crossing my own arms.

"I didn't think you'd take my call if I told you I was hired."

I had the roster before I got here. It was with my official paperwork. The contract that held the terms of my employment here—one that explicitly stated no fraternization with any of the players, many of whom I already know. I studied more film and press on the ones I didn't know than anyone should. But I wanted to know my players.

Lydia has gotten better since I last saw her play. It's not hyperbole to say she was the best player in the league last year.

This time, I drink my fill. From the tight leather pants that showcase that ass of hers perfectly to the pink blouse she's wearing.

Nope. Not going to think of how good she looks right now.

"I can't ignore my coach, can I?" She quirks a brow at me. "Wouldn't make me a very good team player."

"I guess we'll have to figure out how to work together then."

Lydia takes a few steps into the room. A waft of citrus hits my nose. The same perfume she always used to wear. I can still see the clear glass with green liquid sitting on her dresser.

She drops her hands onto her hips. "I have no intentions of *not* working with you. I plan on winning the cup."

"Good. Then we're in agreement."

"Good."

"Great." I smirk back at her. "I guess I'll see you at practice on Monday?"

"What, don't want to catch up?" Lydia tosses her long, blonde hair behind her shoulder.

"From what I can tell, you've been playing hockey these last few years. I think that's all I need to know."

She takes another step closer to me. "But what about you? I don't know anything you've been doing since I last saw you."

Recovering from my injury. Trying to find a new life for myself. Not think about you.

Normal things.

"Hockey," I tell her.

"Well, I guess we have that in common then."

"And now the Rosebuds."

Lydia backs out of the office. After turning, she throws one last glance back at me. "I'll see you around, Coach."

Chapter Five

LYDIA

"Alright. Cheers to the Rosebuds."

Glasses clink together as I knock back the shot of cinnamon vodka. It burns on the way down, but right now? I need it.

"To the Rosebuds!" Skylar and Parker echo.

It's early afternoon, so the bar we found near the rink isn't crowded. Girl Power & Pints is a tribute to women's sports. Even though the city just got a women's team, they have the women's basketball team covering the walls. A few photos of the Canadian women's hockey team are spread out here and there, but considering how dominant the basketball team is, they take up every open wall space. Hell, even the video games in the corner feature them. Hopefully that will be us one day.

We're occupying a high-top table, a bowl of pretzels resting between us.

"I have to tell you, I was so happy to see both of your names when I got traded here," Parker says, smacking her lips together.

"Me too," Skylar says. "Even though I'm still nervous to be here."

"At least you have someone that moved here with you," I tell her. "I feel like that always makes the adjustment easier."

"Okay. Skylar is dating someone. I'm not and not looking," Parker points out. "How about you, Lydia? Are you looking for anyone?"

"No. I don't need anything serious during the season."

"But you told Skylar you knew our coach?" Parker asks, waggling her eyebrows at me. "How exactly did you *know* her?"

I can't help but snort a laugh at her. "Parker, can I just tell you that you and I are going to be great friends?"

She smiles at me in response. "Don't I know it."

"Hey, don't leave me out," Skylar cuts in.

"We won't. Trust me." I smile at her.

"Back to the question at hand." Parker steers the conversation back to where she wants it. "How do you know our coach?"

Those eyebrows of hers waggle again at me.

"Stop it." I wave her off, spotting the server and ordering us another round. "We used to play together."

Do I feel good about lying to her when we just met? No. But what am I supposed to say? My mind is still spinning from seeing Delaney again after all these years, and I might not be as over her as I thought.

Normally, I'm much cooler than this. Because of the chaotic lifestyle of a professional hockey player, I always favored casual relationships instead of anything more serious.

I dated in Boston. I had fun. But hockey has always been the focus in my life.

It was the same when Delaney and I were together. It wasn't serious. It was easy because we were always together. Delaney was the first woman I ever had sex with. I knew I liked women before her, but I had never met anyone like her.

Still haven't. There have been other men and women since, but I don't know why I'm so bothered seeing her again.

Maybe because I never got closure? One day she was there and the next, she was gone.

"That's it? That's the story?" Skylar asks. "It seemed much juicier than that."

I smile at her, sipping on my drink. "Sorry. It's not. We used to play together. We were friends." With benefits, but I leave that part off. I don't need to hint at our history together. "I haven't talked to her in…God, five years? Not since she got injured."

"You were there for it?" Skylar winces, grabbing her fresh margarita and taking a drink. "I remember seeing it after and it was awful."

I nod. "It was. You never want to see anyone go down like that."

"That had to have been hard." Parker leans back, drinking her dark beer.

"I wouldn't wish it on my worst enemy."

"Well, hey." Parker holds up her glass. "Cheers to our coach then and cheers to being teammates."

"Cheers." I smile at both of them before sipping on my own vodka tonic. This will be my last drink if I plan on getting in a workout tomorrow. Preseason doesn't officially start until next week, but once it does, no more drinking for me. I want to be in tip-top shape—mind and body—to be the best player I can be for my teammates. For these ladies that are becoming fast friends.

"You think we're going to kick ass this year?" Parker asks, leaning back in her chair.

I rap my knuckles on the table. "Let's hope. The Rosebuds put together a good team."

Skylar snickers next to me. "Can we talk about that team name? I mean, the Rosebuds? Couldn't they have decided on something better?"

"It's not even a full rose," Parker points out. "It's a bud. It hasn't even bloomed."

"Well, then, we'll have to show them that we're the best team out there," I tell them. "Buds be damned."

"You're too nice," Parker throws back at me.

I shrug, sipping my drink. "I think people here are happy that Toronto *finally* has a women's team."

"Took them long enough." Skylar shakes her head.

"Think we'll ever be this popular?" Parker circles a finger in front of her, indicating the bar around us.

"Fuck yes," I tell her. "We'll be more popular in no time. At least we have better colors."

"Really. Pink and green go better together than orange and black." Parker laughs.

"You know, I was nervous when I got traded," Skylar confesses. "But being out tonight makes it much better."

"You were?" I ask, grabbing a pretzel from the bowl the waiter brought out to us earlier.

She nods. "Making friends is hard for me. I get shy around big groups of new people."

"You were fine around us," Parker tells her.

"Because it was only you two."

I clap my hand over hers that rests on the table. "Well, you've got us on your side."

"Thanks. We'll need to make these nights a regular thing now that we're all in town."

"I agree," Parker interjects. "I could use some girl-friends here."

My phone buzzes in my pocket. Pulling it out, an email pops up on my phone.

From my dad's secretary.

Dear Miss Bishop,

I will pass along your message when Mr. Bishop arrives back in the office. He is out of the office and does not wish to be bothered unless for important reasons.

Regards,

Miss Brennan

I HUFF A LAUGH, shaking my head.

"Everything okay?" Skylar asks, licking the rim of her glass before sipping on her margarita.

"It's fine. Just an email from my dad's secretary."

"Not a good one, from the sound of it," Parker notes, flagging down the bartender to order another beer. "You want another drink?"

"I'm good." I shake my head. "I don't talk to him much."

More like I can't get him to talk to me, but I don't need to get into that right now. I think the last time I talked to him was when I left the national team. I was still living in San Diego then, and had managed to get a few minutes with him at his office.

Have I heard from him since? A few responses to texts every now and then, but nothing big.

"Sorry. That sucks," Parker states, oh so eloquently.

"It's okay. I have my mom and an amazing stepdad that more than make up for him."

I just wish I could shake the feelings that he always seems to stir up inside me. I've wanted for nothing in my life. I have a great family. I love my mom and Derek. So why? Why does he keep making me feel like I'm missing something?

"I could use another shot," I tell them. Even though I said I wouldn't have one, I need one.

"My kinda girl." Parker winks at me before hopping off her chair and running over toward the bar.

"Do you think we're going to have to keep her in check?" Skylar laughs.

I chuckle to myself, grabbing the glass of water on the table and taking a gulp. "Probably. But she'll be fun."

"As long as she doesn't do it before a game." Skylar points a pink-tipped fingernail at me.

"Ooh." I grab her hand and look at her manicure. Half are green with roses painted on them and the others are pink. "This is a great manicure."

"Okay, you're going to have to come with me to my place. It's the perfect pampering after a hard game."

"Done."

"What's done?" Parker returns, holding six shots in her hands with ease. No wonder she's such a good goalie. With skills like that? She can stop anything.

"She's taking me to her nail place."

"Something for you two then." Parker passes out the shots and we down them quickly.

The rest of the afternoon goes by in a blur of more

drinks, shared appetizers, and sharing hockey stories from the teams we came from.

"Listen. If we keep going, tomorrow is not going to be pleasant. And I want to get another training session in before we start practice," Parker says.

"Okay, okay," Skylar agrees. "Probably wouldn't look good to have three of the Rosebuds' newest players too drunk to get home."

"Hey." I point a finger at her as we walk to the bar to settle our tab. "I live close by. You're welcome to crash at my place anytime."

Skylar grins at me. After hanging out with her and Parker all afternoon, I know these two are going to be like sisters to me.

It makes me eager to get started. To get to know more of the women on the team. Making friends is something I've never struggled with. When I started travel hockey, I loved meeting people from all different parts of the country. All three of us head outside together, exchanging phone numbers and starting a group chat.

"See you Monday?" I ask.

"See you then," Skylar says.

"Can't wait." Parker is grinning back at me.

I hug each of them goodbye and head off into the cool Toronto evening. Leaves are starting to change as they rustle in the breeze.

I'm still getting used to the area, but it's nice the bar is within walking distance of the rink and home. My new favorite part about the city? Getting to detour to walk along the waterfront.

The city is bustling. I love it here. It has the same energy as Boston. Every person I've met has been nothing but kind.

Even though I have to figure out how to play for Delaney without thinking about what we used to have, I push that thought from my head.

That's a problem for future Lydia.

Chapter Six

DELANEY

It's late. Too late.

And I'm lying on the hardwood floor in my empty house.

Not a single piece of furniture or box. I landed in Toronto the day before the press conference and stayed in a hotel until the moving company got everything here. I was told they'd be here three hours ago. Checking my phone, I see no pending notifications.

Nothing.

"Am I just expected to stay in an empty house?" I shout in frustration, my voice echoing around the living room. At this point, it's just a room. Who would want to live in here with nothing in it?

Standing, I start pacing the first floor.

I bought this house after doing a virtual tour. Natural hardwood floors. Big windows that overlook the main road. The living room, complete with a fireplace that will be perfect for Toronto winters, flows into the modern kitchen. My favorite part is the walk-out patio with backyard. I can't believe I found something this perfect so close to the rink.

With the primary bedroom upstairs with a large walk-in closet and bathroom any person would dream of having, it was the perfect place.

If only it had furniture.

My phone buzzes in my hand. Sliding my thumb across the screen, I only glance at the caller ID before answering.

"Hello?"

"Ms. Charles?" the older male voice asks on the other end of the line.

"This is she."

"This is Andy from Movers International. I hate to tell you that your truck is delayed."

"How delayed?" I ask.

I know it's delayed, but I don't point that out to him. They were supposed to drop it off earlier. I have practice starting in two days. The last thing I need to be worrying about is getting my house in order.

"It should be here in two days."

"Two days. Is that as soon as it can get here? I have practice on Monday and can't get away to meet the movers."

Fuck. This is not how I want to start my time here in Toronto.

"Sorry, ma'am. But Monday is the earliest it'll be here."

I scrub a hand over my forehead, walking toward the back of my house and opening the sliding glass door.

Darkness is already starting to settle over the city. A cold breeze hits my face, blowing my short, dark hair against my cheeks.

I take a deep breath, trying not to take my anger out on this person. It's not their fault there's a delay.

"Can we at least schedule it for later in the day?"

I mentally walk through my schedule, knowing exactly what time practice will be over. We have just over two weeks of practice and camps before the season starts.

That should be my only focus. Now I'm going to be stressing about making sure my house is livable.

"What time works best for you?" he asks.

"Can we say six?"

"Sure. Seven is the latest we can deliver, so that should be enough time."

"Thank you. I appreciate your help."

"Have a nice evening."

He ends the call and I pocket my phone.

I suck in a deep breath and hold it for a few seconds. The only thing I have in my house is two suitcases worth of clothes and a bag containing my hockey skates.

I guess I'll do the one thing that will calm my head.

Skating.

I grab the black bag and my car keys and head to the rink. The GM and owner have made the ice and workout facilities available to the team whenever they need. A perk of the job I love.

While I don't live far from the rink, the trip takes almost twice the amount of time it should because of traffic. Something I miss about Vermont. Even on the busy days, it didn't take long to get anywhere.

There are a few stray cars still in the lot by the time I get to the rink.

My new home away from home.

Given that it's after usual hours, it's quiet as I enter in my code to the side door and head down the long, cement tunnel behind the ice.

Harsh overhead lights glare off the ice as it comes into view.

Breathing in the cold air, I step out of my tennis shoes and into my skates. The ice crunches beneath my skates as I push off, circling the rink. A gleaming sheet of ice just for me.

It doesn't matter what's going on in my life. Being on the ice is the one thing that always seems to calm me down.

No furniture? No problem.

Stress about the first practice? It'll be okay.

Worry about the team winning?

Nothing that being on the ice can't fix.

Ever since I accepted the position, all I've been thinking about is doing a good job for these women. It's not like they asked to be traded from their old teams. They had relationships with them. A shorthand while out on the ice with their old teammates. Hell, some are even brand-new to the league. I feel like I have to prove myself to them.

I mean, does any man feel like they have to prove themselves when they get a head coaching job or is it only me?

No. They can be mediocre and be in that position for years. Hell, that was what happened at my old college before he finally got fired and I got promoted. After that, the pressure was on.

It's self-added pressure, but I want to do my best for everyone around me. To let them know that I'm a good coach and will help them win.

"I shouldn't be surprised you're out here."

Spinning on my skates, stumbling a fraction, I take a look at the woman now skating toward me.

Of fucking course.

Lydia is here.

Skating toward me in her white skates—the same ones she loves wearing when she's not at practice or a game—a bright smile sits on her face. There's no trace of any makeup.

This is how I always liked her best.

Happy and carefree.

"I could say the same thing of you."

Now that I'm standing still, the cool air feels good against my warm cheeks. Deep grooves line the ice. I wonder how long I've been out here.

"Would you believe I'm working on my form?" Lydia spins in a circle, leaning against the boards in front of me.

"You? Really?" I fight the urge to take in her body. The tight leggings. The black top that clings to her.

Nope. I do not need to be focusing on those things.

"Fine." Lydia pushes off the boards and glides around the ice. I'm helpless to follow her. "I'm getting excited for practice to start so figured I'd come work out some nerves."

Long, blonde hair flows down her back as she moves around the ice with the grace of an angel.

"You were always hard to peel off the ice," I tell her, blowing by her. "I guess some things haven't changed."

Lydia moves around me, spinning to skate backward, staring me down. "You still remember things about me?"

Her words feel like a test. Am I supposed to remember these things about her? Probably not. Yet, I remember everything about this woman. More than I should.

How easy she was to give me a smile.

To make laugh.

How good she felt under me.

But Lydia is against the rules. *No fraternization* flashes in big red lights in my brain.

"You were always the first person in the door for practice and the last one out. It seems like nothing's changed."

She shrugs her shoulder. "What can I say? I like being the best student in class."

"You always did."

"I've got a lot of competition this year though. Toronto put together a good team," she says.

"They did."

I skate past her again, an awkward silence falling between us.

"Are we ever going to talk about what happened between us?"

I fight the groan. "Lydia, it was five years ago. Do we—"

"Have to? Yes."

She stops in front of me and I nearly barrel over her. Lydia catches me, holding on to my elbows to steady me.

This close, her blue eyes are staring up at me. Questioning. Searching.

The last thing I want to do is talk about me ditching her. It's not something I'm proud of. But I didn't have it in me to focus on anything except myself and my recovery.

I told myself we weren't serious. That Lydia wouldn't care and we were just using each other as a means to an end. Mutual orgasms and all.

"What's there to discuss?" I ask casually, not wanting to have this discussion tonight. The very last thing I need is for Lydia to get into my head.

"I mean, I'd love to know why you decided to ghost me. The last time I saw you, you were injured. After that? You were gone."

"We were never serious," I retort.

"I know that," she tells me. "But we still had something. A phone call would have been nice."

It was not my finest moment; I know that. Looking down, I pick at one of my nails, not wanting to look her in the eye. That might be a little too hard. I remember seeing her in the hospital after my injury and the look of panic on her face. That told me all I needed to know right there. And after that, it was just too much for me. I went home and kept to my little bubble.

"Look, Lydia, I'm sorry. Was it the best way to handle things? No. But it was all I could do to focus on myself."

Don't be rattled, Delaney. It's fine. You're having the conversation. It *needed* to happen. We can't let the past fester and stew between us until it explodes. Having it now is better than on the ice in front of other people.

"Thank you."

"Thank you?" I question.

I couldn't have heard her right. *Thank you?*

"Yeah. Thank you." She holds out her hand. "That's all I wanted. An apology."

I take her hand and ignore the way it feels. "Then if you're good, I'm good."

"Good."

"Great," I tell her, ripping my hand away and starting to move around the ice again.

God damn it, Delaney. Stop feeling these things.

Lydia is not your future. She's your past. Sure, what we had was explosive and fiery at the time, but that was only because we were a lot younger and had our whole lives in front of us. Now we have jobs and responsibilities. People to think about. Hell, the only thing I'm going to be thinking about for the next couple of years is my job. I mean all I want—all I've ever wanted—is to lead this team. And now that I finally got it, I don't want to lose it.

This is not how I pictured my evening going. A glass of

wine while unpacking my house? Yes. A conversation with Lydia about our past? No.

"Listen. I'm going to head out," Lydia tells me. "I'll see you at practice on Monday, Coach."

I give her a small smile. "See you Monday."

My eyes trail after her as she leaves the ice, focusing on the generous curve of her ass. I blow out a breath. So much for calming my thoughts.

I need to shift my priorities back to what they should be.

Drills. Film. Lines. Assessing players. That's the only thing I need to be focusing on. The only thing that matters. This team and winning.

You can do this. You've got this.

You've done harder things than this.

Like getting over Lydia the first time.

Chapter Seven

LYDIA

My alarm goes off and I silence my phone, shoving the last bite of eggs in my mouth before grabbing my smoothie to wash them down. The excitement was thrumming through me so I couldn't sleep.

It's finally here. The very first practice of the new season for the Toronto Rosebuds.

There is nothing I love more than the first day of practice. With all the change in the offseason, I'm ready to get back to the thing I love. To the thing I'm good at.

Tying my hair back into a ponytail, I grab my jacket and bag, stuff my feet into my shoes, and pick up my keys.

I blast a playlist to get me even more pumped for practice as I make the short drive to the arena. I crack the windows, letting the cold morning air cool my overheated skin. It's always like this on the first day of a new season.

It's a clean slate. A fresh start for every team and every player. Boston lost in the first round of the playoffs last year. I still haven't won the cup. I'm hoping that will change this year.

Finding the players' lot, I steer my car into an empty

space and grab my bag. The arena is old. Nothing fancy or new like the men's team.

But I don't care. It's ours. My new home away from home.

"Good morning, ma'am." An older gentleman with salt and pepper hair sits at the desk as I walk inside.

"Good morning." I stick my hand out to the security guard. "Lydia Bishop."

"Larry. Pleased to meet you, Miss Bishop. Ready for the season to start?"

I nod. "Yes. I'm excited."

"Me too." He grins at me. "My wife and I were excited when we finally got a women's team."

"I hope we do you both proud."

He nods. "You will. Now, go get to practice so we can win the cup."

"That's the plan." I smack the desk he's sitting behind. "Have a good one, Larry."

"You too, miss."

Walking through the maze of halls to the locker room, the walls are covered in our sponsors' logos. In time, I'm hoping pictures of us playing will replace them.

By the time I get to the locker room, music is blaring. I'm not the only one that is excited to get things started.

"Lydia. Hey." Parker waves me over to where she's suiting up with Skylar next to her.

"Hey. How's it going?" I drop my bag onto the wooden bench next to where Parker is sitting.

"Ready to get this show on the road," Parker says.

"Did you have a nice weekend?" Skylar asks as she pulls her jersey on over her pads.

I smile. "I did. You?"

"Brian and I found a cute new coffee place near us. It feels like we're settling in."

"I'm glad," I tell her.

I don't go into details about my weekend. They don't need to know about my run-in with our coach. Or the conversation the two of us had about our past.

It feels like a new beginning for the two of us. One as a player and a coach.

I start pulling things out of my bag to change into my gear.

"Good morning, everyone," Delaney's voice echoes around the bright locker room.

"Morning," voices reply.

"I'm glad to see you're all here early."

I pull my jersey over my head and pull my ponytail out before facing her. Her eyes are scanning the locker room. She's in a black quarter-zip pullover with the Rosebuds logo on the chest. A matching hat covers her dark bob. With the whistle hanging around her neck, she looks like a professional.

Damn.

It shouldn't be a turn-on to see her like this, but it is.

You're not allowed to have feelings for your coach, Lydia.

Delaney is off-limits. Players and coaches aren't allowed to be in relationships. Not that I have feelings for D. I mean, having a nickname for her does not equate to feelings. None at all.

"Practice starts in twenty minutes, so make sure you're on the ice and ready to go. There's some breakfast in the kitchen in case anyone needs to grab some last-minute fuel. We'll see you out there."

Delaney and the assistant coaches head out. My eyes follow her until she's gone.

"I'm going to go grab something. I was too nervous to eat earlier," Parker says. "You two want anything?"

"I'm good." I shake my head.

"No, thanks," Skylar says.

Grabbing the tape from my bag, I start to wrap my stick. It's the first thing I do before the first practice. Before every game. I can't help myself. I have to do it.

I'm superstitious.

"I'll see you out there?" Skylar is ready to go, stick and helmet in hand.

"See you out there."

The locker room starts to empty as I take a few minutes to settle myself. I don't know what will happen today, but I'm excited.

Excited for this new chapter in my life. For this new group of women I'll be playing with. Hell, even excited to be playing for my ex.

The two of us will be nothing but professional. Based on how she was when I first saw her, I have no doubt she'll keep me at arms' length.

Again, it's fine.

She's my coach. I'm the player.

I'm here for hockey, not Delaney.

Tossing my tape onto the shelf above my locker, I grab my helmet and head out onto the ice. Pucks hitting the back of the net greet me. Skates crunching through the ice.

There's no better sound in the world than hockey.

Parker is in the other goal, scraping the ice in the crease.

I do a few laps around the boards before the whistle blows.

"Alright, everyone. We're going to scrimmage today. Ten minutes then we're going to change up the lines. I want to see how everyone plays together. No pressure. I want everyone to have fun today. Bailey and Nadia have the lineups."

They call out everyone's names and I take my position in my line. As soon as everyone is set, the whistle blows.

Every single thought flees my head as my focus narrows solely to the puck and what I need to do. The center on our line wins the puck drop and passes it to me. I take off down the ice. Skylar is moving with me. I shoot the puck to her. She bounces it back to our center. The defenders are able to hook their stick and get in the way of the pass as they move toward their end of the ice.

Shifting gears, I chase them down and watch as our defenders block a shot on goal. Skylar scoops the puck up and flies down the ice. Watching her skate is a thing of beauty.

Her gaze flits to mine as I accept her pass and put it in the back of the net.

"Great pass!" I call over to Skylar.

I can see her smile through the mask of her helmet.

"That was a great shot." We bump our gloves together as the whistle blows.

"Well done, ladies. Don't get used to that," the goalie tells us. Parker is on our team and at the other end of the ice.

"There's plenty more where that came from."

We skate back to center ice as play resumes. Everyone starts to settle into their lines as we exchange shots on goal. Parker makes a quick glove save then Skylar's shot on the other end is batted away by the goalie's stick.

The whistle blows, ending our time on the ice as we all skate to the bench.

"Nice job out there," Delaney tells us as we take a seat.

"Thanks, Coach," I tell her.

Grabbing a water bottle, I take a swig and watch the game unfold in front of my eyes. The coaches are making notes on their tablets, chatting with each other. Everyone is calling out words of encouragement as scrimmage continues.

Damn. I have no idea where the lines are going to end up, but everyone looks good.

It's only the first day but it makes me excited to be a part of this team. To be a part of something special.

Don't get me wrong—I loved what I had in Boston. It was the first professional team I played for after I left the national team.

Now that I have a few years under my belt, it feels like I can take a real leadership role on this team. With so much new talent on the team, this is what I want. Hell, maybe I can even become captain.

As the final whistle blows after a good, hard practice, I can't wipe the grin off my face.

It's going to be one hell of a season for the Rosebuds.

Chapter Eight

I can breathe a sigh of relief. The first practice of the season is always the one I worry about. It sets the tone for the rest of the year. Having a group of women playing together for the first time? You never know what you're going to get.

But after mixing up the lines today, I've got a feeling that we have something special brewing.

I watched the women that have been in the league for years help those that were called up with the expansion.

"Hey." Bailey, one of my assistant coaches, knocks on my door. "Want to grab dinner with Nadia and me tonight?"

With fiery red hair and freckles, I remember Bailey from my playing days. She was one of Canada's greatest players to ever play the game. Everyone thought she quit at the peak of her career, but she wanted to move into coaching.

I'm thankful we snatched her up.

"I wish I could, but I have to go home and wait for my furniture to be delivered."

Her hazel eyes go wide. "Are you sleeping on the floor?"

I shake my head. "No. I grabbed a hotel room. I'm too old to sleep on the floor."

Bailey bursts out laughing. "Definitely not in our college years anymore where we could sleep anywhere."

"Don't I know it." I smile back at her. "Sorry I won't be able to join you."

"Unless you want some help?" Bailey asks.

"You want to help me move?" I lean back in my chair, crossing my arms.

"Call it bonding."

Standing, I lock my tablet and put it into my bag to take home with me. "If you really want to help me move, I will take you up on that."

"Great. You have anything to drink? Moving is made better with beer."

Laughter spills out of me. "Beer and vodka."

"My kind of girl."

"Do you think Nadia will want to help?" I ask.

"Nadia is my partner. She'll come."

"Wow. You have no idea how much of a help that will be."

Maybe if I'd planned better, I wouldn't be in this situation. Since I walked off the plane here in Toronto, I've had tunnel vision. Yes, I've met my assistant coaches, but I've been so hard at work getting ready for this day, that I've ignored everything else.

I throw the strap over my shoulder and follow Bailey out of my office and hand her my phone.

"Text me and I'll send you my address. Anything you're allergic to?"

"No, we're both good."

"Great. I'll order a bunch of food for us to snack on."

"Awesome. See you soon."

I smile as I head toward my SUV. I was planning on having to unpack everything myself, but I'm happy for the help and the company. On the way home to meet the movers, I call the local pub down the road to order delivery.

Pretzels and cheese. Buffalo wings. Artichoke dip. Pizza rolls.

Everything to make moving and unpacking boxes better.

By the time I'm pulling into my small driveway after studying film and drawing up some more lines for practice tomorrow in my office this afternoon, the moving van is there.

Thank God.

"Miss Charles?" the young man asks, jumping out of the cab of the truck.

"That's me."

"Great. Ready to get started?"

"Yes. I appreciate you coming later."

Unlocking the front door, I swing it open so they can start moving everything in. With four of them, they start with the furniture, taking it where I direct.

"There's a reason they made you the coach." Nadia laughs as she and Bailey follow my mattress into the house.

"Hey, I want to make sure it goes in the right room. I won't have time to move it later."

"Well, I'm glad they're starting because we grabbed the food from the delivery driver out front."

Bailey holds up two large plastic bags and hands them to me.

"Thank God. I'm starving."

Setting them on the counter, I start to take out all of the containers and crack them open. With no plates yet, I hand out sets of plastic forks to divvy up the food.

"Pizza rolls?" Bailey questions.

"What do you have against pizza rolls?" I laugh. "They are bite-sized pockets of deliciousness."

"Nothing. I'm just surprised the bar had them." She takes a hearty bite as Nadia takes a seat on one of the barstools.

"Okay, beer for both of you?" I ask, grabbing a pizza roll and stuffing it in my mouth.

"What are you having?" Nadia asks.

"Dirty Shirley."

"Interesting." Nadia smirks.

"What?" I grab a pretzel and dunk it into the dip.

Is there anything better than a hot pretzel and cheese?

"Just not what I expected from you. I figured you'd be a bourbon or scotch woman."

"I like cherries. What can I say?"

"I'll take one of those," Nadia tells me.

She's a striking woman. Even though Nadia is short, with a dark pixie cut and wide brown eyes, she is a force to be reckoned with.

Handing each of them their drinks, I hold my glass up in a cheers.

"Thank you both for helping me. I know this is probably not what you thought you were going to do tonight, but I really appreciate it."

"What are friends for?" Bailey smiles at me. "But we need a getting to know you activity."

"Wait, seriously?" I choke over the bite of dip I just put in my mouth.

"I agree with Bailey," Nadia says. "All we know about you is that you coached at VU before being named head coach of the Rosebuds."

"We want to know the good stuff." Bailey rubs her hands together.

"Well, what is it you want to know?" I ask, taking a carrot stick and dunking it in the ranch.

"Are you dating anyone?" Nadia asks.

I shake my head. "No."

Except that I hate the first thought that comes to mind is Lydia.

"Do you want to be dating someone?" Bailey asks. "We know a lot of nice people we could set you up with."

"As much as I'd like to get to know a nice woman, I'm okay. Hockey first."

Nadia bumps her elbow against Bailey's. "That's how this one was until we met. You'll find the right person at the right time."

I nod, grabbing another pretzel and dipping it into the hot cheese. "Well, unless I meet them at the rink, I doubt I'll be finding anyone anytime soon. I feel like I need to prove my worth to the team."

Nadia waves me off. "You'll do it. Trust me. Both of us felt it today."

"Yeah? Because I did too."

The team looked great. Every year with Vermont, I always start with a scrimmage. Mixing the lines gives me the best chance to see strengths and weaknesses. How they best work together.

"Hey. Here's to a great season ahead." Bailey holds her beer up and we each toast her. "We've got a good team together and I think we can go far."

"Knock on wood." Nadia raps her knuckles against the table. "We don't want to jinx it."

"That is the one thing I don't buy into," I tell her.

"An unsuperstitious hockey player? I didn't think they

existed." Nadia laughs, grabbing a wing and tearing into it. As we're chatting, boxes marked KITCHEN are set in a stack against the wall. "Should we get started on those?"

I nod, grabbing a napkin and wiping my hands off.

"Back to this *you not being superstitious*," Bailey says, ripping open the top box. "Plates and bowls. Where do you want these?"

I spin on my heel, assessing my kitchen. "Cabinet next to the refrigerator. And I'm not superstitious because if we have the talent and work hard, there's no reason we won't go far."

"Okay, that's fair," Nadia says. "But what if the other team is just as good?"

She starts handing dishes over to Bailey as she puts them away. I grab another box of glasses and find a cabinet for them.

"That means we have to work harder. Learn their weaknesses to beat them."

"Wow," Bailey says. "You really are a coach. But you're never going to convince Nadia not to be that way."

"Sorry. Not going to happen." Nadia smiles at me.

The two of them share a familiar smile. One of comfort, like they've been together for a long time.

"So how long have you two been together?"

"Three years now?" Nadia asks. "Has it been that long?"

"Do you have to ask?" Bailey questions.

"Well, is it three years? Because we weren't official for six months or so."

"Uh-oh." I break down the box and rest it against the counter. "I hope I didn't start something."

"We disagree on this a lot. We always decide on two and a half years," Bailey clarifies.

Nadia rolls her eyes, mouthing three to me.

I snicker, starting on a new box. Listening to these two go back and forth, I know I'm going to like them. One of the things that I always found hard with hockey and traveling around was making friends.

When I met Lydia, we connected on the first day. I felt lucky to have made a new friend. Once I got to know her, I saw how easy it was for her to make friends. Something I never had.

So when Bailey volunteered so readily to help? It makes me feel lucky that I'm going to have these two in my corner.

"Are you thinking of the game over there?" Bailey asks, chucking a balled-up piece of packing paper at me.

"What? No."

"You totally were." She laughs. "You really are all about hockey."

"Seattle does have last season's second highest scorer," I tell them.

"And the first was Lydia." Nadia's eyes gleam. "And we've got her."

"Damn straight," Bailey says. "Did you ever play with her?"

I nod. "For a few years. Until I got injured."

"I'm sorry that happened to you," Nadia says. "That had to have been hard."

"ACL and MCL? You seemed to make lemonade out of lemons," Bailey tells me.

"Not how I wanted to end my career, but I didn't want to become bitter. I always planned on coaching. It just sped up my timeline."

"And hopefully we can bring home a cup or two together," Bailey says.

"Hey! Knock—"

"On wood," Bailey interrupts Nadia. "We know."

"Okay, I'll let you have that one." I smile at them.

"Oh, thank God. I can't change." She fake wipes her brow.

With the kitchen almost done between the three of us working, and the food annihilated, I tell them, "You really don't have to stay. I can finish up the living room tomorrow."

"Are you sure?" Bailey asks. "It's still early."

Glancing at my phone, it's almost ten. "This is early for you? Damn, I'm getting old."

"You're what, thirty?" Bailey asks. "Nadia is a spring chicken here at twenty-six."

I laugh. "Thirty-six. And I'm usually in bed by this time. Early practice and all."

"Well, we're happy to stay if you want us to."

I shake my head. "I'm okay. You can head home. Do whatever spring chickens do."

"Like a face mask with a warm cup of tea," Nadia says. "I need to be ready for practice tomorrow."

"I appreciate that." I point a knowing finger at her. "I'm really thankful you two helped."

They both come and give me a hug. "Anytime you need anything, just let us know."

"Same. Whatever you need, you have my number."

They grab their bags and jackets and walk out. I wave the two of them off, closing the door behind them. Boxes are still strewn around the living room. I'll have to get my bed made and dig out some clothes for tomorrow. But having one room done takes a huge load off my shoulders.

Especially since it was done with friends.

I'm glad these two are going to be my assistant coaches. Having real friends here is going to help occupy my brain. Keep it from focusing *only* on hockey. Or Lydia.

That last one is something I really don't need to be thinking about.

Lydia. Lydia only.

Damnit.

Hockey. Hockey has to be the priority.

Now if I keep telling myself that, maybe I can believe it.

Chapter Nine

LYDIA

"You ready, sis?" Troy asks. "Big night for you."

"She knows it's a big night," Angie's voice rings out, tinny on the speaker phone in my tiny bathroom.

"I'm ready," I tell them.

"And you have your outfit ready to go?" Angie asks.

"You know I do."

It's perfect. Every bit of this is perfect for my first walk-in as a Toronto Rosebud.

The light pink corset-style top is covered with bright pink embroidered roses. They spread over the entire front and over the sheer, short sleeves. Paired with a pair of wide-leg green pants, it's just right for the first home game.

"I can't wait to see it," she tells me. "You know I'll be looking at pictures during the Black Diamonds game tonight."

"Hey!" Troy's voice shouts. "You need to watch my game."

"I'll be lucky to watch ten minutes with how much this baby makes me have to pee," she whines. "I don't like you both playing on the same night. It's harder to pay attention."

"It's okay," I tell her. "You can watch Troy. Even if I'm the better player."

"Ouch," his voice comes over the line. "And on that note. I have to head out. Good luck, Lyd. Love you."

"Love you guys."

I end the call, smiling to myself at the two of them. Troy has always been one of the most supportive people of me playing hockey. My real dad? He was supportive until it became too much when I was a teenager. I wish he showed more interest because…well, look at me now. Helping launch a brand-new team in Toronto and hoping to make a name for myself here.

Grabbing my lip gloss, I swipe on one last coat before heading out. Music blares from the speakers when I turn the car on and make the short drive. I love the first game of the season. Playing at home against one of the new expansion teams allows us to show our city what we're made of.

Seattle. I know a few of the women on the team. One of my old teammates from Boston is their newest defender.

Since I'm a winger, we'll have plenty of time together on the ice. It's going to be fun to see how the season plays out.

We've had a good few weeks of practice. The team is meshing well on and off the ice. Something that I think is made easier with a good coach.

Which Delaney is. I'm not surprised at all by it. She has the temperament and patience to go a long way in this league.

Pulling into the parking lot, I turn the car off and get ready for my first walk-in.

This is one of my favorite parts of the game. The

energy walking in feels like a living, breathing thing. It helps me get hyped and in the right headspace.

"Good luck tonight, Ms. Bishop," Larry, our security guard says to me as I walk by.

"Thanks. It's going to be a good one tonight."

"Hopefully in favor of the Rosebuds."

"Fingers crossed." I smile at him as I start the walk down the tunnel.

Flashbulbs are popping as I walk through the tunnel that leads toward the locker room. The press are calling out for me as I wave to them.

"Great look, Lydia. How do you feel about the first game tonight for the Rosebuds?"

"Thanks. I'm excited," I tell the one reporter. I don't recognize her yet. After a few games, I'll know her. I like getting to know them. Having the press on your side makes things easier.

"Hey, Lyd. You look great!" Skylar calls out to me, waiting halfway down the tunnel.

I jog down to her. "Not as good as you. You look amazing."

"Thanks." She tucks a lock of curly, brown hair behind her ear.

In a tight leather skirt and an oversized, white flowy top, she looks stunning.

"You ready for the game tonight?" I link my arm through hers as we head toward the locker room.

"Yes. I need to get this nervous energy out. First game always sets the tone for the rest of the year."

"We've got this." Pushing open the door to the locker room, a few people are already here. Some are stretching. Others are doing yoga. Since it's early, dinner sits in chafing dishes on the tables for all of us.

"I'm glad that we get to play at home. I can't wait for our fans to see us play."

"Me too."

From what the team has told us, there was a high number of season tickets sold. Even more single game tickets for tonight. I want to show off what we've got to the city that's done nothing but support us since day one.

"Hey, ladies," Parker's voice calls out to us as we grab some dinner.

"Hey. You ready, goalie?" Skylar bumps shoulders with her.

"You know it. Seattle won't know what hit them."

My jersey hangs in my locker. The green material has Rosebud patches on it—with a pink C patch on the left chest.

It was an honor to get voted captain by my teammates. I want to make them and my family proud.

Also on that jersey is my familiar number.

Twenty-two.

Derek's old number.

It's the only number I've ever worn. The same number Troy wears. I'm thankful I was able to get this same number here.

My nerves are bouncing around inside me as I change into my gear. It's that antsy energy before a game when I can't wait to get out onto the ice.

As everyone starts to filter into the locker room, I start the process of taping my stick. This time in a bright pink for the first game of the season.

By the time it's taped to my liking, everyone else is ready to head out to the ice for warm-ups.

We're greeted by fans cheering for us. Even though it's a smaller arena, the stands are filled. They're crowded around the glass as we do laps on our end, shooting pucks at the goal.

Excited fans are holding up signs. I wave to them as I do more laps before starting to stretch. Seeing the little girls wearing Toronto jerseys makes me want to do them proud. I wish there had been a league like this when I was their age. I remember Derek taking us to watch the high school team play, but they didn't have a women's team.

Boos echo around the arena as Seattle's team makes their entrance. The corner of my mouth tugs up into a smile. I know a lot of the women playing for the Sirens. Some of them I remember from my junior days.

As we continue our warm-ups, more and more people take their seats. Music fills the arena as Skylar and I pass the puck back and forth. Fans are chanting for the Rosebuds.

I fucking love it.

By the time we head back to the locker room for the Zamboni to clean the ice, it's hard to wait for the game to finally start.

"Alright, everyone. Can I have your attention for a minute?" Delaney calls our attention to her. "The first game of the season is here. I know we've all been looking forward to it."

The assistant coaches flank her. She looks impeccable in her suit.

"I'm proud of all the hard work you've been putting in during practice these last few weeks. Seattle is a good team, but we have what it takes to go far." She glances to look at Nadia, who smiles back at her. "But let's take it one game at a time. Go out there and play the hockey that I know you can play."

"Rosebuds on three!" Bailey comes into the center of the room and we all follow suit. "One, two.."

"Rosebuds!"

The pregame announcements are a blur before I'm taking my position on the ice. The puck drops and our center grabs it with ease.

She sends it to Skylar, who passes it across the ice to me. Scooping it up, I fly down the ice before deking out the defender and shooting it to Skylar.

Dodging another defender, she sends it back to me before I send it toward the goal. Seattle's goaltender blocks it off her stick, their defender grabbing the puck and taking off.

Our defenders are waiting for them as they enter their attacking zone. We're chasing them down, but Parker is ready. She snatches the puck with her glove, stopping their first goal attempt.

The whistle blows, stopping the play.

"Way to go!" I shout to Parker.

Seattle wins the face-off, but our defenders are there. They pass the puck to Skylar who is moving toward our zone. I'm skate for skate with her.

She fires the puck at the goal. It ricochets off the bar, but I'm there to rebound it into the cradle of my stick and send it flying into the back of the net.

The horn blares and the crowd erupts.

"Yes!" I throw my arms up in the air as Skylar skates over to hug me.

"Way to go, babe. That was amazing."

"All you," I tell her, clapping her on the helmet.

"Nice one, Bishop."

"First goal of the season."

All the women are congratulating me as we skate back to the bench for the line change.

"Great job, Lydia," Delaney tells me as I take my seat.

"Thanks, Coach."

I don't have to hide my grin from her. Shy away from her praise or attention. Because I'm fucking ecstatic.

First goal of the season? It feels good to have it under my belt so early in the first period. To not have the pressure on my shoulders to score.

The entire game is a battle. Seattle is good.

We're better.

Parker is the star of the game, blocking and batting away every shot that comes her way. Skylar is able to put another goal on the board in the middle of the second period, and I finish it off in the third.

We seal the win, 3-0.

After shaking hands with the Sirens, I skate to where Parker is waiting.

"Shutout? You're incredible!"

I wrap an arm around her as Skylar joins us.

"Parker White! You were amazing tonight. I'm so proud of you!"

A shutout to start the season? Shutouts are hard-won in this league. I couldn't have asked for more.

"You two helped seal the win."

"You did," I fire back.

The three of us head back to the locker room with happy smiles on our faces.

The press is waiting for us for postgame interviews. It's easy to answer the questions when we came out on top.

Questions answered, I hit the showers and get cleaned up. By the time I'm walking back into the locker room, Delaney is making the rounds, offering kind words to every player.

"Parker, great job out there tonight. You were on fire," she tells her.

"Thanks, Coach."

"And Lydia." She turns to me, holding her hand out, eyes firmly focused on mine. "First goal of the season."

I take what she gives me—the game puck.

"Thanks, Coach." The way her fingers brush mine sends heat coursing through my body. I lock eyes with her, giving her an easy smile. "Hopefully the first of many."

"Keep it up."

She pulls her hand away, leaving nothing but goose bumps in her wake. Turning to my locker, I pull on my clothes as Delaney starts her postgame speech.

"That was a great team win! Great job, Parker, on shutting Seattle out. Not an easy thing to do. Way to start the season off on the right foot. Everyone looked good out there. Skating. Passing. It all looked great. There are a few things we can clean up, but we're off to a promising start. Montreal is coming up, and they have a good looking team. Enjoy the first win tonight, and I'll see you all tomorrow for practice."

Claps and cheers ring out as people start to head out.

"I'll see you two tomorrow?" Skylar asks. "Brian is going to take me out to celebrate our game."

"Sounds good. I'm going to call my parents on the way home," I tell them.

"Glad I'm not alone in that," Parker adds. "I'll see you tomorrow."

They both head out together, leaving me alone in the locker room.

Me and Delaney.

"You looked good out there, Lydia," she tells me.

She's leaning against the doorjamb of the hall that leads to her office.

"Thanks. Felt good to get back on the ice."

Smiling, Delaney walks over to me. "I haven't seen you play in years. You've gotten better."

"I should hope so." I return her smile. "I love the game too much to not get better."

"It's noticeable. I love that you're having fun out there."

"Helps that I'm playing for a good coach." I wink at her.

"You make my job easy."

Grabbing my bag, I sling it over my shoulder. "I plan on keeping it that way, D."

"Coach," she retorts. "In here, I'm Coach."

"Got it. And out there?" I nod my head toward the door.

"Delaney."

"No nicknames, got it."

Delaney takes a few steps back, putting distance between us. "Get a good night's sleep. You'll need it for practice tomorrow."

"Got it. See you then, *Coach*."

Because that's all she'll ever be to me.

My coach.

That's it. Nothing more.

Chapter Ten

DELANEY

"Alright, everyone. Before we leave, I want to tell you what a great game that was. I know that some of you are heading off for international tournaments, but I want us to carry this momentum into the break. I wish you all the best of luck, and for those who will be staying in Toronto, we'll be having a few light practices that are optional, but I strongly encourage you to attend."

"Yes, Coach," everyone says in unison.

I smile at the group and head to the back of the bus. Bailey and Nadia stay up front, but I like the back. With most of the women congregated to the front, sitting back there gives me more room to spread out and watch film on the ride home.

I hate that the professional league has a break so soon after the season starts. Leading the league at 3-0, I don't want our momentum to come to a grinding halt. It's not like we didn't have breaks at the collegiate level, but they at least came at a time when the break was needed to give bodies a rest.

"Before we get going, can I say something?" Lydia pops up from her seat halfway back.

"Floor is yours."

I brush past her and take my seat, watching as she turns her back to me.

"Thanks. I know this isn't an official team event, but I'm going to be working with one of the local shelters to host puppy yoga this weekend. If anyone is interested, we'd love to have you. The more people that come, the better chance we have at getting these puppies adopted."

A few people raise their hands, letting her know they'll be going.

I fight the groan. Why does Lydia Bishop have to be the most perfect woman? Not only is she one of the best players on the team, she's now helping puppies get adopted?

If this woman has a flaw, I can't find it.

Happy chatter filters back as I pull out my tablet to start studying game film for our first opponent after the break.

Playing New York, with at least five of their women heading to Europe for the upcoming tournament, I'm hoping we'll be able to take advantage of their jet lag to catch them off guard when we head down to play them.

We only have three of our players gone, thankfully.

"Do you ever take a break?"

Lydia pops up over the seat in front of me, staring at the tablet in my hand.

The cabin lights are off, with only a few overhead lights shining down. It's gotten quieter, with people no doubt popping in headphones for the drive home. Even though it was an afternoon game, by the time we pulled out of the rink, darkness settled over the city.

"There will be a time for breaks later."

I pause the footage of New York's game from earlier this week. Even though they won, I can still glean a lot from how they played.

Like seeing how they became less aggressive as the game went on, even though they were only up by two goals.

"Still the same old Delaney."

Stepping into the aisle, Lydia takes the seat across the aisle from me and crosses one leg over the other. My eyes move on their own, taking in the patterned tights and long black sweater dress she's wearing. She looks effortlessly sexy.

"I figure I might as well get it in now since the team is sending me down to Florida to do some scouting."

"Really?" She gives me a questioning look. "Don't they have actual scouts to do that?"

"Not this time. Since we're on break, and the team scouts are headed to Europe, they're sending me. She's a college player with a lot of potential."

Lydia drops her elbow onto the armrest and rests her chin in her palm. "I guess we're both going down there then."

"What are you doing down there?"

"I've got a photoshoot with one of my new sponsors," she tells me.

I lock my tablet and set it on the seat next to me. There's no harm in talking to one of my players, right? "What company?"

"Island Siren. It's a new sustainable swimsuit company bought by a woman billionaire out in Seattle. I'm really excited for it."

"That sounds exciting," I tell her.

What I don't tell her is that I can easily imagine her in said swimsuits. Or *not* in the swimsuits.

Why does this woman make it so hard to be around her?

"It's my first big sponsorship, so I hope they like me." The confession slips from her before she can take it back.

"Who wouldn't like you?" I blurt out. "You're easy to like."

Talking to my player? Yes, that's okay. Telling her that? Probably *not* okay.

Lydia gives me a coy smile. "Does that mean you like me?"

"You're my player. Of course I like you. I like all my players," I backtrack. This conversation is heading to the danger zone. And fast.

"I do too," Lydia agrees. "I also like all my coaches."

"Even when they point out things you're doing wrong?"

That cuts the flirty tension between the two of us when shock colors her face.

"What am I doing wrong?" she asks, ignoring where our conversation was going.

"You want to know?"

"Yes. If I need to improve my game, I want to know."

I laugh. "And you're telling me to take a break?"

"As you said, I'm your player. Coach me."

"Fine." I grab the tablet and power it on. "Late in the game, especially close ones, your stickhandling starts to get a bit…"—I try to find the right word, one that won't offend her—"lax."

"Lax? Let me see."

I tap on the video of her playing our game against Montreal and queue it up for her.

"You skate hard, Lydia. It's not in every game that—"

"Damn it," she interrupts, ignoring me. "I thought I was getting better at that."

I study her as her eyes flit over the small screen that casts her features in a dim glow. Even though it's been a long time since I've seen her, she is still one of the most expressive people I've ever met.

And based on her reaction now? She's annoyed with herself.

"Guess I'll be at the rink tomorrow working on stickhandling. I can't be slowing down when the team needs me."

I laugh and take the tablet away from her, much to her dismay. "I'm not telling you this so you can get to the rink tomorrow to fix it. Just something to be aware of."

Lydia leans back in the seat, crossing her arms. "I did tell you to coach me."

"It is why they hired me."

"I guess I'm going to have to work harder. I don't want to let my coach down. I mean, none of us do."

I bury my own reaction by busying myself with tucking the tablet away in my bag. I don't miss the note of pride in her voice. Or the way it does things to my insides. Things that should definitely not be happening because of who she is.

Lydia was my past. *Is* my past. We have no future together.

I'm her coach. She's my player. There is no realm in which this would work.

"I'm assuming you'll be at the rink tomorrow?" Lydia asks, drawing my attention back to her.

"Where else would I be?" I smile at her.

"Good. Then that means you can help me with my skills. Maybe a little one-on-one?" She stands, ready to go back to her seat.

I know what she means, but that damn flirty tone is

back. The implication of her words sends waves of heat through me.

Stop it!

I cannot be thinking about her like this. I'm back in the danger zone. The area where things are gray and Lydia isn't my player and I'm not her coach.

Where I want things to happen that shouldn't be happening.

"I'll see you tomorrow." With a wink, she's gone, giving me back what little willpower I have left around her. I need to find it, build up a resistance to her, because I cannot keep having these feelings for her.

It's not like I can talk to Bailey or Nadia about it. Or my mom. I just need to find the strength to build my walls up to her to be able to resist her.

I can do it, right?

Chapter Eleven

LYDIA

"**M**mm. That feels so good," I purr. "Don't stop. I'm so close."

"I love how responsive you are to me. Such a good girl."

"Yes. Always. I love your touch."

My body aches. Drips with need. The slide of her tongue inside my pussy curls my toes. My fingers slide into her dark hair, needing more.

"Aren't you greedy? Wanting more."

"*Needing* more," I correct her.

When two fingers are thrust inside me and that tongue flits over my clit, I'm damn near ready to explode.

"Come on my tongue, Lyd. I'm ready for it."

"Delaney—"

"Holy shit!" I startle awake, popping up onto my elbows to find the woman who was ready to make me come.

Except I'm alone. The room is dark except for a sliver of light coming from the edge of the blinds. My body is a live wire ready to snap, nipples so hard they could cut glass.

Because I had a sex dream about Delaney.

My coach.

Fuck. This is the last thing I need to have happen.

I flop back onto the bed, frustrated and angry because I was so damn close to coming. There is no way I can go to practice this wound up.

There's only one thing I can do about it.

Reaching over to my nightstand table, I fish my vibrator out of the drawer and turn it on. Buzzing fills the quiet room.

Thank fuck the thing is charged.

Hooking my thumbs in the waistband of my shorts, I toss them to the side. Sliding the suction head over my clit, immediate relief floods my body. I tweak my nipples through the soft satin of my camisole while picturing a woman between my legs.

It doesn't matter who. It's the tongue that's sliding between my folds. Sucking on my clit.

God. It's been too long since I've had sex. Turning the strength up, I dig my heels into the mattress as I get closer and closer to tipping over the edge.

A moan slips out as I imagine those fingers curling inside me. The delicious combination of hand and tongue pulls me into the abyss when familiar brown eyes flash across my vision.

"Oh fuck. Fuck!" I shout.

I can't control it. It's Delaney's face I'm picturing as I come. Her sexy smile. Eyes filled with desire. Mouth drinking up every drop of my release.

Oh God. What have I done?

How is it I came harder at the *thought* of someone than I have at a real person's touch in ages? Taking several deep breaths, I start to come down from the high. Turning off the vibrator, I toss it on the bed.

At least I don't feel as wound up as I did when I woke up. That has to count for something.

Except…

How am I going to face Delaney—my coach—at training today when it was *her* I was picturing? When it was *her* that brought me to orgasm?

I am so fucking screwed.

X.

I WASTE no time grabbing my gear and making a beeline straight for the ice. This will be easy. I can make it through today like an adult and not worry about interacting with Delaney.

I'm the first one here. No surprise. Which means the ice is a blank slate. Completely clean just for me.

There is no better feeling than fresh ice as I tear across it. The grinding and slicing of my skates as I push myself harder and faster. Needing to work out these feelings that have awoken inside of me.

Maybe I'm focusing too much on hockey. The puppy yoga will do me some good this weekend. Get out there. Meet new people.

As it is right now, the only people I know here play or coach for the Rosebuds. And one of my neighbors that I bumped into on the way over today. A nice, older woman who was taking her dog out for a walk.

Reaching one end of the ice, I swerve around the goal and take off in the other direction.

My cheeks are cold as I stop on the opposite red line. This time, I skate to the blue line and back before heading toward center ice. It's one of the worst drills in hockey, but right now, it's the only thing distracting me.

I'm starting to feel the burn in my legs as I keep driving myself across the ice.

"Hey."

"What?" I jump back, nearly knocked off my skates as Delaney skates over to me. Skylar is with her, starting to glide across the ice to settle in.

"Are you okay?" She studies me with a quizzical eye.

"I'm fine." If fine means I had a sex dream about you and can't stop thinking about it, then I'm fine. "Just fine."

"You sure?"

"Sorry. You scared me. I didn't hear you come in."

She looks down at the ice. "Clearly. You've been here a while."

Deep grooves are cut into the ice from my skates. "Oh, sorry. Couldn't sleep so I thought I'd get a head start."

"And here I thought you were trying to wear yourself out so you'd be able to work on your stickhandling skills."

The smile she gives does nothing to help quell the thoughts I'm having about her.

She's your coach. She's your coach.

If I say it to myself another hundred times, it might start to sink in.

"Right. That."

She gives me a quizzical look before grabbing one of the pucks. "Let's go ahead and get started. Head to the other end of the ice and I'll start sending them to you and then you shoot them to Skylar."

Skylar smiles at me. "Let's do it."

"I don't want your stick going a foot outside your skates. If it's outside that zone, let it go. I know it's basic, but sometimes, the most basic drills help."

"Got it."

Taking a deep, cold breath of air, I skate to the opposite end of the ice. Having some distance helps push her from my mind. Instead, I focus on the tiny rubber disk she sends my way.

Grabbing it with the cradle of my stick, I send it toward Skylar who sends it to Delaney. Who is already sending another puck my way.

It's more and more of this. Repetitive to the point of boredom, but it helps me keep my attention on the matter at hand.

The pucks are flying. Some too wide to hit, others right in the zone.

"That's a great start," Delaney tells the two of us. "Sometimes we get too in our heads and lose sight of the puck during the game. If you can do this when you're tired, it's really going to help you during the game."

"Thanks, Coach," Skylar tells her. "We'll keep working on it."

"Great." Delaney gives her a smile. "Feel free to come in whenever you'd like during the break, but make sure to take some time for yourself." She looks at me. "Both of you."

"Got it," I confirm. I don't know how much relaxing I'm going to be able to do thinking about Delaney, but I can sure as hell try.

"Good morning, everyone." A deep, booming voice echoing in the empty rink has the three of us spinning toward the bench.

The general manager, an older man with dark brown hair and a graying mustache, looks onto the ice with a proud grin. We skate over to where he's waiting.

"Mr. Tremblay. It's nice to see you," Delaney tells him.

"Nice to see you're all here during the break."

"Nowhere else I'd rather be," Skylar says, beaming at him.

"Glad to hear it." He turns to where Delaney is standing in front of me. "I'm glad I caught you today."

"Is everything okay?" she asks, hesitant.

"Oh yes. I wanted to let you know there has been a last-minute change in plans for the scouting trip next week."

"Is it still on?" Delaney asks.

"Yes, yes. But seeing as how Miss Bishop's sponsor is flying her down, they've offered to give you a ride."

"Oh." Delaney looks to me, as if to see if this is okay.

"Works for me." I plaster a fake smile on my face.

"Good. You'll both be in the same hotel to make things easier. Island Siren has arranged a car service to pick you up, and Delaney, since you're traveling with Miss Bishop now, they have also added you to the dinner reservations once you arrive."

"I appreciate you taking care of all of this," Delaney tells him.

"Anything to make the trip easy. I'm looking forward to getting your thoughts on this new player," Mr. Tremblay says.

"I watched her film last night. She's good. I think she'd make a great addition to the team," Delaney says.

I can't help but smile. Of course Delaney has studied film on this potential recruit. It's the one way the two of us are alike. We live and breathe hockey. We can't help it.

"Good." Mr. Tremblay looks at the three of us again. "I won't bother you any longer. Keep up the good work, ladies. You're doing the Rosebud name proud."

I watch as he leaves before Skylar starts doing laps around the ice.

"Sorry," Delaney whispers once it's the two of us.

"For what?"

"For getting dropped onto your trip like that."

I shrug a shoulder, because what else can I do?

"It's fine. Totally fine."

After today, that word is going to lose all meaning.

I thought I would get at least some breathing room from Delaney over the break.

Turns out, I might not get that at all.

Chapter Twelve

LYDIA

"Okay, when you said we were going to be doing puppy yoga, I didn't think it was going to be this much fun."

I laugh at Parker.

"We haven't even started yet."

"But look at all the dogs!"

Walking farther into the local gym where the yoga class will be taking place, a mass of people are swarming around what I can only assume are the dogs.

A tiny chocolate lab breaks free, running to greet us.

"Look at you." Parker scoops him into her arms, pressing kisses onto his head. "Isn't he the cutest?"

"That's a she, and she's a feisty one." A woman jogs over to us, cheeks pink. "Sorry. People keep taking them out of the playpen before we start. It's like they want to get away from me."

"Are you Jane?" I ask, sticking my hand out. "I'm Lydia."

"Oh, Lydia. It's so nice to meet you. I'm so glad you reached out to do this."

"I'm happy to. I've never gotten to do anything like this before."

"I promise, you'll love it." She waves at us to follow her. "Do you want to meet all the dogs?"

"Yes," I tell her. Parker ignores her, cooing all over the puppy in her arms. "I think you might have an adoption already."

"She's mine," Parker says, ignoring us as she drops down onto one of the mats to play with her.

"That was easy." Jane laughs. "But in all seriousness, thank you. Events like this help get our name out there and make it easier to find forever homes for these precious babies."

Jane looks to be around my age, with blonde hair that is laced with hot pink, and bright, hazel eyes.

"Whatever you need from me to help, not just today, but whenever, just let me know."

"I really appreciate it."

A crowd of people are beneath the basketball hoops, clustered around a makeshift fence.

At least a dozen dogs are inside. Some have their paws up to get a closer look at the people staring at them, others are snoozing, while others are playing with each other.

Finding an opening, a small, yellow lab spots me and darts over to me.

"Hi there. What's your name?"

His tongue hangs out of his mouth as I rub behind his ears.

"This is Buddy," Jane tells me. "He's almost old enough to be adopted."

"What's that mean?"

"He's got two weeks before he's old enough, but I didn't want to leave him behind. He'll go home with me to his mom, but then if someone is interested in him today, they can pick him up in a few weeks," she says.

"Where'd you find him?" I ask, rubbing his belly as he rolls over on the ground.

"His mom was running around on the street when we found her. She gave birth a few days after we rescued her. So sad, but all the puppies are okay. The rest of his litter mates have already been adopted."

"What about his mom?"

Jane smiles at me. "I'm keeping her. We bonded and I just can't let her go."

"Aww, that's sweet. Well, I don't know if I'm going to be able to let this little guy go."

"I can get you an application to fill out, but if everything checks out, he can be yours."

"Yeah?" I ask.

"Definitely. It's the whole reason we're here today. Want to take him over to your mat for yoga?"

"Yes."

Picking him up, Jane puts him in my arms as I spot Parker, now with Skylar on the mat next to her.

"Sorry I'm late," Skylar says in way of greeting when I reach them. Her eyes are red-rimmed and a lopsided ponytail is falling out. "It's been a morning."

"Are you okay?" I ask, concern for my friend buzzing through me.

"Eh. Brian isn't adjusting well here." Her lip quivers as I take a seat next to her.

"Here. Play with Buddy. He'll make you feel better."

Her sad eyes light up when I pass the tiny yellow lab into her lap. "Oh, he is cute. Is he up for adoption?"

"Not anymore," I tell her, scratching behind his ears.

She laughs. "How did I know you were going to go home with a dog?"

"Hey. I'm not the only one." I point behind her to where Parker is sitting with her dog. "Parker beat me to the punch."

"I mean, who can say no to this little face?" Parker coos.

"Do you have a yard for her?" Skylar asks.

"Yes," Parker says.

"I mean, I have a massive patio for him, but I can picture going on runs with Buddy here," I say, rubbing his back.

"Does he like to run?" Skylar asks.

"He will. Maybe I can bring him to practice and he can be the team dog."

"What's this about a team dog?"

I startle at the voice behind me.

Delaney.

"Hey, Coach. We were thinking our dogs can be the team mascots." Parker holds up her puppy.

Delaney laughs, walking over to her and the pup in her arms. "This hasn't even started and you've already adopted a dog?"

"She found me," Parker says. "It was meant to be."

"What about you two?" Delaney asks.

"No dog for me." Skylar sighs.

"I'm going to take this guy home once he's old enough." I press a kiss to the top of Buddy's head. He turns back, trying to chomp my chin with his baby teeth. "Might need to change his name though."

"What is it?" Delaney asks.

"Buddy. I think he needs something more inspired. What are you going to call her?" I ask.

"Her name is Truffle. I think I might stick with that."

"Hi, sorry to interrupt." Jane comes back over to us. "The instructor wanted me to let you know that we'll be starting in just a few minutes, so to grab a mat and get ready."

"Thank you," I tell her.

"Mind if I take this empty one?" Delaney asks.

"Not at all. I'm surprised to see you here," I say.

"I figured since so many of you were coming that it would be a good way to support you."

"Even if we're getting team dogs?" Parker chimes in from her spot.

"I don't know about that." She laughs.

Skylar hands Buddy to me, but I wave her off. "You can keep him for now. I think you need him more than I do."

"Thanks."

Toeing out of my shoes, I slip out of my coat and drop it at the top of my mat. Eyeing Delaney next to me, I watch as she does the same. It's hard not to watch her.

She was—*is*—the most gorgeous woman I've ever met. In a black workout bra and black leggings with X's cut out along the side, it's hard not to take notice of her.

Even though she's no longer playing, it's obvious to see she's still in shape. Her biceps flex as she pulls her dark bob back into a low ponytail. The thin material clings to every inch of her. Her toes are painted a bright red.

Delaney is even more sexy now than when the two of us played together. I can't seem to take my eyes off her.

"Thank you everyone for being here today," the yoga instructor calls out. "I want to give a special thank you to Lydia Bishop and the Rosebuds for helping to put this event on. I'm hopeful that with all of you here, we can get a good workout in while also getting some of these dogs adopted."

Buddy hops between my mat and Skylar's, sniffing at my shoes and coat.

"Be a good boy and don't eat those," I tell him, pushing the shoes out of his way. Instead, he goes to gnaw on my hand.

"Someone likes you," Delaney tells me as our instructor keeps talking.

"Today is going to be free flowing, free movement. Feel free to follow along with me, but if something feels good and you want to stay there longer, please do." One of the dogs yelps and bounds up to her, stretching his paws against her legs. "What do you think? Do you want to start with downward dog?"

Everyone laughs as she starts going through the movements.

Yoga isn't something that is in my normal workout routine, but every time I do it, it feels amazing. I follow the instructor as she leads us through the moves. They aren't hard, but as Buddy wiggles between my feet, he makes it hard to balance.

"Now let's move into sphinx pose."

Dropping onto my stomach, I push up onto my elbows. This, Buddy finds, is the perfect height to attack my face with kisses.

"Buddy. Stop. I can't focus."

But he doesn't. Probably because I'm laughing as he keeps going.

"Did you expect this to happen?" Delaney asks, peering one eye over at me.

"This? Not really."

"It means he likes you." There's a smile curling the corner of her mouth as she looks at the two of us.

"He's easy to like."

Delaney goes to speak, but is cut off by the instructor.

"Let's go into warrior two."

Buddy circles the empty space below me and flops down on a sigh.

"Must be hard being that cute," Skylar says. "If only I could get one."

"Later," I tell her, hating how sad she sounds.

She goes back to her moves and I do the same. My eyes keep glancing around the room, seeing all the happy faces as puppies play with each other and the people around them.

"This was a great idea," Delaney tells me as we finish in child's pose.

I turn to face her, seeing her smiling at me. It does funny things to my insides. Until Buddy pounces on my chest.

"I hope I can do another one."

"Are you going to become the dog lady?" Delaney laughs, standing and rolling up the yoga mat. She grabs mine from me as I slip into my shoes and pick up my new dog.

"Just the one for now. Buddy deserves all my attention."

"I'd ask if you'll have more balance getting a dog now, but I think I have my answer." Delaney and I each give Buddy one last scratch behind the ears as I hand him back over to Jane.

"He'll be in good hands until you can get him," Jane tells me. "Thank you again. We have applications from a lot of the people here today, and some are even interested in our older dogs."

"I'm so glad. It was a great day."

"Thanks."

I head back to grab my things, waving goodbye to Skylar and Parker.

"Honestly? It'll probably be all Biscuit and hockey

now," I tell Delaney, answering her question from before I dropped him off with Jane.

"Biscuit?"

I nod. "He doesn't seem like a Buddy. More of a Biscuit."

"Keeping it hockey related. I should have known."

"What can I say? I'm a creature of habit." I slide into my jacket and zip it up, standing outside the gym.

"I guess I'll see you Monday?" Delaney asks.

"See you then."

What I don't tell her?

I can't wait to spend uninterrupted alone time with her.

Being around Delaney is dangerous.

But I just can't find it in me to care.

Chapter Thirteen

LYDIA

LYDIA

Meet the newest member of the family
<<picture of Biscuit here>>

TROY

You adopted a dog?!

ANGIE

Oh my God, Lyd! He is so cute!

DEREK

Do you have time for a dog?

MOM

And in your apartment?

Yes. The adoption coordinator came out
yesterday since I'm leaving today and said
it would be more than enough room for him

TROY

Can we get a dog, Ang?

ANGIE

Baby first, then a dog

TROY

Damn

ANGIE

What's his name?

TROY

You should name him after your favorite hockey player, Troy something…Hollins maybe?

I can't name him Lydia. That would be too confusing

TROY

Ouch!

ANGIE

Yes! Go Lydia!

TROY

Hey, you're supposed to be on my side!

And this is why Angie is my favorite

TROY

Rude

MOM

What are you calling him?

DEREK

Way to change the subject, dear 😏

MOM

I try 😬

Biscuit

TROY

Fitting

TROY

Troy would have been a good second choice

DEREK

Or tenth 😅

TROY

Gee, thanks Dad

TROY

See if I give you grandpa of the year award

I'll definitely be aunt of year

TROY

Maybe

ANGIE

You totally will 🩶

TROY

You're killing me, Ang

ANGIE

Love you too

Gotta go! Off to Miami 🌴✈️

I'll send more pics when I get Biscuit

MOM

Have a safe trip. Love you

DEREK

Safe travels. Love you, Lydia

ANGIE

Have fun at the shoot! Can't wait to see pictures

Thanks! Take care of my niece 😽

"Hey."

Stuffing my phone in my bag, I look up to see Delaney in front of me in the private terminal for our flight.

Standing in a lightweight Rosebuds jacket that goes to her knees, her face is bare of makeup and a Rosebuds knit cap covers her head.

"Hey."

"Looking at cute pictures of your dog?" She smirks.

"More like telling my family I'm getting a dog."

"You got approved then?"

"Yeah. Jane came over yesterday to do a walkthrough. Only two weeks until he'll be ready, and I'll be able to bring Biscuit home."

"That's great."

"Excuse me, Miss Bishop?" A young woman in a pencil skirt and blazer walks up to us. "We're ready to depart if you'd care to follow me to the plane."

"Thank you."

Wheeling our bags behind us, we follow her to where a smaller jet is waiting by the hangar.

"This is what you get with your new sponsorship?" Delaney asks, jaw dropping.

"I wasn't planning on this. I would have been just fine on a big ol' commercial plane."

We head up the narrow stairs to the plane, and once we're inside, another crew member takes our bags and stows them for us. There's one couch and a few seats lining the aisle.

"Can I get either of you something to drink for the flight?" our attendant asks us.

"I'll take a glass of champagne if you have any." I'll need something to settle my nerves. Not only for the flight but for being in a cramped space with Delaney for the next three hours.

"A Dirty Shirley?" Delaney asks.

"Coming right up." She smiles at both of us as we pick seats across from each other.

"I see some things haven't changed," I say.

Unzipping my jacket, I stuff it into the small compartment overhead and take my seat.

"What can I say? I like what I like."

Delaney is sitting in her seat, eyes raking over me. *Is it getting hot in here, or is it just me?*

I opted for a pair of leggings and a black cropped top paired with an oversized cardigan to travel in. I shed the cardigan, needing to cool off.

"I won't disturb you, but if you need anything, just press the call button. I'm up front with the pilots," our flight attendant tells us as she brings our drinks.

"Thank you so much."

"Has anything changed since I last saw you?" I ask Delaney, double-checking to make sure my seatbelt is securely fastened as we take off down the runway.

I guess the one upside to traveling by private jet is there's no waiting in line. Which means my nerves don't have time to unseat themselves.

She smiles at me. "I see nothing has changed with you."

"Hey." I point a finger at her. "Having a healthy fear of planes is completely normal."

"Is that why you're breaking your 'no drinking during the season' rule?" She nods to the glass in my hand.

I take a sip. "Yes. It helps with the nerves."

"Is the flight the only thing triggering your nerves right now?"

She smiles at me. The one that I always missed when

she left. It's soft, happy. Like she's privy to a secret that not many know about me.

"What else would make me nervous?" I quirk a brow at her. The plane lifts from the ground, the city falling away around us.

"Can I confess something?" Delaney asks, sipping on her drink.

"Yes."

A finger circles the rim of her glass. "Being around you makes me nervous."

"Really? Why?"

"I mean, like here." She waves a finger around the plane. "At the rink? I'm cool as a cucumber. But just the two of us? It feels…"

"More intimate?" I finish for her.

"Yeah." She lets out a breathy sigh before taking another sip of her drink.

Dirty thoughts lodge themselves in my head. What I wouldn't give to lean over to taste that sweet drink on her lips. To taste the cherries.

With only the two of us in the cabin on this plane, I could do whatever I want right now. But Delaney? She's the rule follower.

I don't want her to reject me. I lost her once. Being shot down again? I don't know if I could take it.

Again, I shouldn't even be entertaining the idea. It's against the league's no fraternization policy.

"Then let's talk about something…not intimate."

"Like what?" Delaney brings her legs up onto the seat, turning to face me fully.

"Like…" I grab my bag from the seat and fish around for what I'm looking for. "Friendship bracelets?"

Delaney's laughter echoes around the cabin as we start to level off. "You still make those?"

"What?" I scoff. "They are fun to make."

"And distract you from the flight." She shakes her head. "I'm glad some things haven't changed."

Friendship bracelets—the old-school kind made with thread—was my way to make friends when playing hockey growing up. There weren't that many girls' leagues in Southern California. Travel was a regular part of life growing up.

Because of it, I met more people than I ever could have imagined. Which is why I loved making friends with all the girls I played with.

"Do you still have the one I made for you?" I ask, starting to make complicated knots in the thread.

"Maybe…"

"I'm going to take that as a yes," I say, separating the threads and hooking it around the notch on the back of the seat in front of me.

I like to think that she still has a small piece of me. Even though we didn't part on the best of terms, I never stopped thinking of her.

Out of nowhere, the plane takes an unexpected dip. It doesn't stop shaking as we hit a patch of turbulence.

"Sorry, ladies. We've got some rough air coming up for the next thirty minutes or so. Please make sure your seatbelts are fastened," the flight attendant says, popping her head out to let us know.

I grab the belt and tighten mine. Delaney, on the other hand, grabs her bag and drink then unbuckles hers.

"What are you doing?" I ask.

She steps over me, taking the window seat next to me. "Making sure you're okay."

"I don't think that's in your coachly duties," I remind her.

"It's going to be a long flight if you're over here stressing."

Another bump and my hands grab onto the armrests as I squeeze my eyes shut.

"Who says I'm stressed?"

"I do. Now, would you like an actual distraction?"

Turning my head, I peek one eye open at her. "What do you have in mind?"

"Well—"

"And don't say join the mile-high club. We are *not* doing that."

Delaney laughs and it slides over me like honey. God, I missed that sound.

"Don't worry, Lyd. I wasn't going to suggest that." She fishes around in her bag and pulls out a package of markers. "Temporary tattoos."

"You're still doing that?"

Delaney pokes me in the bicep with her colored pen. "Like you, it was always a good distraction. I don't do it as often, but I have them when needed."

"Care to play a game?" I ask, taking the pen from her.

"Tic-tac-toe?" She smiles at me.

"Only if we can do it on you."

Delaney quirks a brow. "Sure."

Pulling up the sleeve of her gray sweater, she rests her arm across the armrest. Taking the red marker, I draw a board on her arm. "You know we can only play once. Unless you want X's and O's drawn all over you."

"Maybe one game. Then you can draw on me."

"I love that you're still doing this." I mark an X in one corner.

"You have your distractions. I have mine."

"Because you're too chicken to get a tattoo." I laugh.

"Okay." Delaney points the pen at me, not before

making an O in the middle of the board. "You have a healthy fear of planes. I have one of needles. I can have a tattoo and it washes off."

"After this, I'm giving you a tattoo."

"Cherries, please."

I make another mark. "That's the tattoo you'd want?"

"Yes. It's sweet and innocent, but sensual."

"Kind of like you."

"Is that how you see me?" she asks.

I draw a line connecting my three X's. "I win. And mostly, but more sensual."

"Are you going to draw my tattoo now?" Delaney asks, a teasing lilt to her voice.

"Where do you want it?"

The bumps of the plane go mostly ignored as she shifts, rolling up the sleeve on her other arm. "Here."

Finding the two markers I need, I start tracing an outline of the cherry stems. Her skin is soft. So damn soft I'm having trouble concentrating.

This is the exact opposite of making things less intimate. Being in this enclosed space. Breathing her air. All it does is make me want her more.

Delaney looks at the drawing on her arm. "You know, if this hockey thing doesn't work out, you could have a future as a tattoo artist."

"You think so? Because that's not exactly an award-winning drawing."

I smile, tracing the poorly drawn stem.

"Eh. I like it because it's from you."

Her dark eyes lock on to mine.

Desire.

Want.

Need.

Her emotions are all over the place. It pulls me in

closer. Drawing me in as her tongue darts out to lick her bottom lip.

Her own eyes flash to my mouth. I bite down onto my lip. I want this. More than anything.

Just as I move even closer, the sound of the overhead chime causes me to jump back into my seat.

"We've found clear skies, ladies. If you'd like, you can unbuckle your seatbelts and I'll bring you some fresh drinks," the flight attendant's voice rings out.

It breaks the swirling tension between the two of us.

"Right." Delaney unclicks her seatbelt. "I should probably get back to studying film."

"Good idea."

She moves over me back to her seat. Headphones securely in place, the video playing on her tablet is the only thing she's paying attention to.

Fuck.

We can't cross that line. We got too close to it.

But I don't know how much longer I'll be able to resist this woman.

Chapter Fourteen

DELANEY

This is dangerous.

The closer and closer we get to the hotel, the harder it is to breathe. I keep thinking about Lydia. Teeth sinking into her bottom lip. What she would taste like. What she'd feel like.

Would it be as good as I remember? Or better?

By the time our car is pulling up to the roundabout entrance of the luxury hotel, the salty sea air is a reprieve to my overly taxed nerves.

Palm trees sway in the distance as a cool breeze blows through. It's just what I need on my warm skin.

"Want to drop our bags off and then meet down in the lobby for dinner?" Lydia asks, an easy smile on her face.

"Are you sure that's a good idea?" I heft my bag onto my shoulder and take my wheeled bag from the valet. I nod in thanks.

"You have to eat, D. It's just a meal."

I stop, pointing a finger at her. "I will only eat with you if you don't call me D."

She smirks. "Okay, *Delaney*."

"Better." I fight the smile. "Let's check in and I'll text you."

"You better."

The check-in line is nonexistent as the two of us each step up to an awaiting employee to get our keys and quickly head to the elevator. I get off on the fifth floor while Lydia takes it up to the seventh.

Finally.

Finally I can breathe Lydia-free air. Free from that sweet vanilla scent. Swiping my key card over the reader, I push open the door.

Wow.

This is better than I imagined. A small sitting area welcomes me. A hallway to the right leads off to the bathroom and bedroom. The floor-to-ceiling windows look out over the water. Dropping my bags, I walk into the bedroom. A patio offers views of the pool deck below.

A gift basket sits on the bed. Grabbing the card, I read the handwritten note.

Miss Charles,

Please enjoy your stay at the Miami Grand Luxe Hotel. Should you require anything, please do not hesitate to reach out to us.

Enjoy!

The Staff at the Miami Grand Luxe

I CAN'T REMEMBER the last time I've stayed anywhere so…fancy. Traveling with hockey teams is a lot of buses and budget hotels. A few days out of the cold in Toronto?

I can handle this.

My phone buzzes in my pocket.

LYDIA

Are you coming?

SAY NO, *Delaney. Say no.* It's the responsible thing to do. Don't get swept up in the idea of Lydia. The Rosebuds are the most important thing.

Not Lydia. No matter how important she was to you at one point.

DELANEY

Coming down now

DAMN IT. My fingers respond before I can stop them.

Great. I've got a table for us and ordered a round of drinks

WELL, so much for doing the responsible thing.

She's my player. I'm her coach. That's it. That's all. We

can share a meal together and it not mean anything more than that.

Grabbing my room key from the foyer desk and a light jacket in case the air conditioning is blasting in the restaurant, I run my fingers through my hair and head down. The hotel is buzzing with people. Some are coming back from the pool, skin pink from the sun. Others are dressed to the nines, ready for a night out on South Beach.

I follow the signs to the restaurant, and when I get there, I am not prepared for what is waiting for me.

Fuck. Me.

Lydia is at a table right in the front. She looks stunning in a black dress with thin straps. Her blonde hair is braided over one shoulder and a smile paints her face.

I didn't give a second thought to changing. At this point, the more clothed I am, the better.

"I'm glad you didn't stand me up," Lydia says as I take my seat across from her.

"Like you said, it's just a meal."

I grab my napkin and lay it across my lap.

"Tell me about the player you're scouting. That's nice dinner conversation."

I smile, grabbing a roll from the basket and dragging it through the oil. The taste of herbs bursts on my tongue. Delicious.

"She's probably the most sought after player at the collegiate level. Could be the next Lydia Bishop."

"Hey. There is only one Lydia Bishop."

"I said could be. We'll see. Good, raw talent, but needs a good coach to help her harness it."

Lydia holds her glass up and I clink mine against hers. "Then let's hope she comes to the Rosebuds. I'd say we have a pretty good coach."

"Stop it."

"What?" She shrugs. "I'm stating the obvious."

"You don't have to kiss my ass." I roll my eyes at her as our waiter comes by.

"Good evening, ladies. Have you had a chance to look at the menu?"

"I'll have the salmon salad," Lydia says.

"Umm." I grab the menu and give it a quick scan. "I'll do the Greek orzo bowl, please."

"Excellent choices."

He leaves the two of us alone. It's still early, the restaurant filling up around us. Tables are crammed together in the space.

As people take the seats around us, my nerves unfurl.

There is nothing remotely sexy about a dinner with strangers sitting on either side of you.

"Are you excited for your big shoot tomorrow?" I ask.

"Yes, but nervous."

"Why? You're going to be a natural."

She drinks from her water glass. "It's the first time I'm going to be doing anything like this."

"Picture it like doing postgame interviews. The press love you. It'll be easy."

"The press are easy," she tells me. "Talking about hockey? That's easy. What if I don't know how to pose? Or if all the photos look terrible?"

"Lydia. You are going to look incredible. They wouldn't have chosen you if they didn't want you. Tell the photographer how you're feeling tomorrow."

"You think so?"

I nod, taking another bite of bread, swallowing before continuing. "You said this is a woman-owned company?"

"Yes."

"Then I have no doubt that she'll be some badass woman who will put you at ease within five minutes."

A slow smile spreads across her mouth. "Thanks, Delaney."

I don't miss the way she says my name. Not my nickname.

See? This is good. You can handle this.

"It's nice to see you like this."

"Like what?"

"Nervous. I don't think I've ever seen you like this. Not even the night before our first game with the women's national team."

"I do get nervous," she points out. "I just don't show it to everyone."

Our meals are set down in front of us and we say our thanks to the server.

"Enjoy. Please let me know if you need anything else."

"It looks great. Thank you."

"It smells delicious." Lydia breathes in her salad, a piece of pink salmon on a bed of greens with oranges around it.

Blackened chicken sits on top of the orzo, with olives and tomatoes mixed in with feta crumbles on top.

An easy silence settles between the two of us as we dive into our meals.

"Excuse me." A little girl comes up to us, a nervous grin on her face. "Are you Lydia Bishop?"

Lydia sets her fork down and scoots closer to her. "I am. What's your name?"

"I'm Emma and I'm your biggest fan. I love hockey."

An older woman stands behind the little girl. Lydia smiles and says, "Me too. Do you play?"

She nods, curls bobbing. "I want to be a hockey player just like you."

"Hopefully you'll be even better if you work really

hard, okay?" She nods. "Do you want a picture and an autograph?"

"Yes, please."

She moves in and her mom snaps a picture as Lydia signs the piece of paper with the hotel logo on it.

"Thank you so much. She spotted you walk in and wanted to come say hi. The Rosebuds are her favorite team."

"I'm so glad you did. Keep up the hard work, Emma," Lydia tells her.

"I will. Thank you!"

She waves as she heads off with her mom.

"How cute was she?" Lydia gushes. "That makes me so excited for when my niece is born."

"Your brother is having a baby?" I ask.

"Yes. I cannot wait to be Aunt Lydia. That girl is going to be so spoiled. And I can't wait to play hockey with her."

I laugh. "Are you going to be able to teach her before your brother does?"

"Probably not. But she'll have plenty of people around her to encourage her."

"You say that like you didn't have people encouraging you." I take another bite of my dinner.

"I wish my dad was more supportive. I'd love to be able to share all of this with him."

"Was he ever supportive?"

She shrugs. "Yes and no. When I was little and playing peewee, it was fine. But once I got better and had a chance to play in college, it didn't work with his schedule. He came to a few games here and there, but it fizzled out in college."

"That has to be hard."

"I wish I didn't care."

I want to reach out and take her hand, but I can't. "It's

only natural to want him to care. Especially when you're going to be the greatest player ever for the PWHL."

"Damn right." The sadness in her voice washes away. "And I'll have the rest of my family cheering me on. Including my new niece."

"Exactly."

A picture of Lydia and me teaching our kids to play hockey flares to life in my mind. It's so real, so visceral, it's like it's already happened. As if it's a memory.

As quick as it comes, it goes. Leaving a sadness in its wake. We won't be able to have that. Not with the positions we're in now.

"You okay?" Lydia asks.

"Just tired is all." I look down at my bowl, no longer hungry. "I might call it a night."

"Oh, okay. Do you want me to head up with you?"

"No. That's okay." I wipe my mouth and set the napkin down. "I'll see you tomorrow morning, okay?"

She gives me a wry smile. "Have a good night."

I leave the restaurant like my ass is on fire. The elevator feels endlessly slow as I wait for it in the lobby. I'm running away like a coward. I have to be around Lydia and have to figure out how to deal with the feelings. Maybe writing them down will help.

As the elevator dings, I step out and walk to my room. With too many thoughts filling my head, I need to get them out. Swiping myself into the room, I grab a pad of paper and a pen.

I have never once stopped thinking
about you since I got injured. I wish I
could, but I can't. You're the one that got

away and it's hard to be around you because I remember what we had. What we can't have now.

But God, if I don't want to kiss you. Want to throw you up against a wall and kiss you senseless. Relearn what you like. What makes you sing.

I want all of it with you.

Even if we can't have it.

I SCRIBBLE IT ALL OUT, ripping it from the pad and stuffing it in my jacket pocket. There are some things Lydia doesn't need to know.

And how I'm feeling is at the top of the list.

Chapter Fifteen

LYDIA

I'm rushing. I shouldn't be. But after tossing and turning all night, I barely slept for an hour.

The elevator is taking forever. I'm only on the seventh floor, but we've stopped on every floor.

I only have a few more minutes to get outside to where the photoshoot is taking place. Thank God I didn't have to do any hair or makeup because that would have made me even more late.

By the time we get to the lobby, I'm darting out of the car.

"Excuse me, ma'am."

I turn to the woman calling me. "Yes?"

"I think you dropped this."

"Umm." I look at it. It's not mine, but I recognize the logo on it.

A Rosebuds jacket.

"Thanks."

"Sure."

I have no doubt that it's Delaney's. Fishing around in

the pocket to see if she left anything in it, like her phone or room key, I pull out a wadded-up piece of paper.

Unfolding it, I know I shouldn't read it, but I can't stop myself.

I have never once stopped thinking about you since I got injured. I wish I could, but I can't. You're the one that got away and it's hard to be around you because I remember what we had. What we can't have now.

But God, if I don't want to kiss you. Want to throw you up against a wall and kiss you senseless. Relearn what you like. What makes you sing.

I want all of it with you.

Even if we can't have it.

HOLY SHIT.

This is how Delaney feels? Is this why she ran out of the restaurant last night? A bump to my shoulder stirs me back to life.

Realizing I'm standing in the middle of the lobby, I follow the signs to the pool deck, shift my iced coffee to my other hand, and pull out my phone.

I TUCK MY PHONE AWAY, no longer nervous about the shoot as I walk along the stone path through the palm trees. Lush plants and flowers line the walkway. The smell of salty, ocean air permeates everything. The happy sounds from the pool hit my ears as I find someone that looks to be in charge.

"Hi. I'm Lydia."

Her smile is bright. "The woman of the hour. I'm Dina. It's so nice to meet you."

"It's nice to finally meet you too."

"I can't tell you how thrilled we are that you're going to be repping our swimwear this upcoming season."

"I can't wait to see what I'll be modeling."

She sweeps her hand in front of me. "We've got hair and makeup ready for you and then we'll let you get changed into your choice of suit to start. Sound good?"

"Sounds great."

A few ladies are already waiting for me. Smiling at them, I take the offered seat and drop my tote bag at my feet.

"You've got your work cut out for you today."

The makeup artist sitting in front of me smiles at me before pinning my hair back. "Please. You make my job easy. We'll make you look gorgeous."

"Thank you."

"Eyes closed, please."

Following her instructions, I sip on my iced coffee to try and wake myself up. I couldn't get the image of Delaney fleeing the restaurant out of my head. I hate that the two of us are in this situation. Having to figure out how to be around one another when it's now obvious that we want each other.

My hair is curled and sprayed. My lips painted and my face covered in various creamy products. I don't normally get pampered like this, but I'm going to enjoy it while I can.

"You're ready to change."

"Really?" I ask, peeping one eye open.

"Yes. Take a look."

She steps to the side and wow. My hair is curled in perfect beach waves. The kind of waves I always dream of but can never seem to perfect on my own. My makeup? It's flawless. The peachy colors of my eye makeup have my blue eyes popping. A light coat of lip gloss was swiped across my lips, but not too heavy.

"Wow. All of you are amazing. I could never do this."

The makeup artist squeezes my shoulder. "You're going to knock them dead. The suits are behind you, so go ahead and change. A robe is on the back of the door. So come out once you're ready."

"Thanks."

After they leave, I stand, walking to the racks of clothes. Pushing the first hanger to the side, I look at the black material of the first top. It's a delicate mesh material in a bustier style. The only coverage is two large, embroidered flowers sewn over the breasts. More delicate flowers decorate the straps and two ribbons tie in the back. With the matching bottom, it is stunning.

The ones next to it are more of the same. Two pink flowers held together with tiny pink straps between the cups. A strapless blue number with a blooming blossom over the bust.

Classy, yet sexy. Nothing overly sexual.

I can't believe that I get to model all of these. This is my first big sponsorship, and getting to be the face of a new major swim line that values eco-friendly fashion while promoting equality in women's sports? It's a dream come true.

I grab the black two-piece and head into the curtained-off area. Slipping off my clothes, I pull the butter-soft material up over my legs, before securing the top as best I can. Turning to face the mirror, my ass looks amazing in this number. I adjust my breasts to fit behind the flower cups. I'll need an extra set of hands to make sure the back bands are tight enough.

The robe is silky soft as I slip it on, and I find a pair of slides to step into before heading out into the sunshine. I find the assistant and follow her toward the group of people on the beach. This area is roped off, leaving it wide open for us to work.

The tide is starting to come in near where the cameras are set up. I can only imagine how great these photos are going to look.

A woman with a gray cropped bob introduces herself to me. "Hi there. I'm Cindy and I'll be your photographer and leading the shoot. If at any point you're uncomfortable, let us know and we'll stop."

Looking around, I notice that everyone here is a woman. "I appreciate that. It's nice to see an all-female crew here."

"Dina's idea. She's a champion of women. It's why I was eager to get this shoot." She looks chagrined. "Well, and to get to meet you. You're my daughter's favorite player."

"Really? I love that. I'm happy to sign something for you."

Her eyes go wide. "That would be amazing. But let's get down to it. The light is amazing and I don't want to lose it."

"Just tell me where to go."

"Have you ever done anything like this before?" Cindy asks.

"I haven't."

"We're going to start with the palm trees." I look to where she's pointed and see a second group of people. "Then we'll change suits and then hit the water. Sound good?"

"Sounds like a plan."

I move over toward the cluster of people underneath the palm trees. Dina is waiting there.

"You look great," Dina tells me.

"Thanks."

"Remember, just have fun with it. You're a sexy badass and everyone is going to love these photos of you."

I smile at her before shrugging out of my robe and tossing it toward her.

"We're going to spray some oil on your skin and give your hair one last fluff and then we'll get started."

"Sounds great."

Oil is sprayed on my arms and legs as the hair stylist teases my hair.

"Okay, on your knees, Lydia."

Cindy slips into professional mode as part of the crew moves my arms around to find a better position. Sand grinds under my knees as I shift around as the camera snaps in front of me.

"Give me more pouting. Yes. That's it! Keep going!" she shouts as I do as she instructs.

It feels weird to have this many people watching what I'm doing, but hearing her encouragement spurs me on.

I bite my lip, trying to look sexy as I tousle my hands in my hair. It doesn't feel natural, but I'm doing what I think they want.

"Think about your partner. A time when you've felt sexy. Yes. Beautiful. Keep going."

I don't tell them that I'm thinking about a certain coach I want. Who still wants me.

Thinking about Delaney is dangerous. Letting my mind stray to how sexy she is to me is *not* what I should be thinking about.

"Whatever you're thinking about, Lydia, keeping thinking it. You're doing great," Cindy says.

"Fabulous. Okay. Let's change out the suits and then we'll head to the water. Sound like a plan?" Dina asks.

"Sounds great."

Clouds are starting to move in as I head back to the changing room to find the blue one-piece suit. By the time

I come back out, it's gray overhead, and we've changed shooting locations.

I follow the same path out and meet Cindy down at the water.

It's more of the same positions and faces, except this time, the water is exploding behind me. I can only imagine how good the photos look.

Salt water clings to every nook and cranny as I lie in the sand. Every minute of this is fun as Cindy continues encouraging me.

Before I get the chance to change into another suit, the skies open up, rain deluging us with water.

Looking up, I throw my hands into the air, relishing this moment. The only thing that would make it better is if Delaney were out here with me right now.

Dashing toward the changing room, everyone is huddled together as Cindy nearly wipes out coming in.

"We might have to postpone the rest for tomorrow." She presses a few buttons on her camera. "But damn, Lydia, the camera loves you."

She holds up the device to show me the tiny screen. Rain is coming down in sheets as I'm looking skyward, the brightest smile on my face. Palm trees are blowing in the wind behind me.

"Holy shit. I love it."

It's completely spontaneous. Unplanned. Candid.

"That might be the photo to lead the campaign." Cindy zooms out, and there, in perfect view, is the blue swimsuit with the flower on it. "Dina. Come look at this."

She appears over my shoulder, staring into the camera. "That's it. I fucking love it. God, thank you. Thank you."

I'm beaming at the two of them. I had no idea how today was going to go, but this? I'm excited about this partnership with Island Siren.

"Thank you for what?"

"For looking incredible. For wanting to partner with me. For the fact that you are going to be a huge inspiration to so many young girls out there that you can be a badass hockey player and showcase your inner *and* outer beauty. Truly, thank you."

I'm blushing at her words.

It's one of the reasons that out of all the sponsorship offers, I chose this one. Not only is it led by a female CEO, but she's a badass and a champion of women everywhere.

"I'm honored you chose me. Thank you."

She hugs me before heading out and dashing back to the hotel.

"I'm glad we allowed for contingencies, because it looks like it's going to be like this all afternoon," Cindy says.

"I guess that means I'm going to have to study film this afternoon then. Gotta get ready for our next game after the break."

"Good. I want you to beat New York."

I laugh. "I'll do my best."

"That's what I like to hear. Enjoy the rest of your afternoon."

"I will."

I guess I might as well drop Delaney's jacket off and study film. It's not like I have anything else going on.

Chapter Sixteen

Is this one of my better ideas? Probably not. But when all I could think about was Lydia and her photoshoot today, I couldn't help myself. Instead of going to watch some of the games being played here this afternoon—the *safe* thing to do—I slipped on my sunglasses and a ball cap and came down to the beach to watch Lydia's shoot.

I don't know what she was worried about because she is stunning.

The two-piece suit she chose was made for her. The high legs make her delicious ass look even more incredible than normal. So good that I want to sink my teeth into it.

With her hair tousled and the wind blowing through it, she looks like a goddess.

A cool breeze starts to come in with the gray clouds. As the camera people start to move, I take that as my cue to head back into the hotel.

Heat and awareness prickle on my skin at how gorgeous Lydia is.

Taking the elevator back up to my room, it's hard to

"

concentrate. The last thing I can focus on is hockey. I need to be studying my recruit and her stats.

But right now? I don't care.

There's only one thing that is going to make this better.

Heading into the bedroom, I dig in my travel bag and find what I need.

My vibrator.

Thank God.

Slipping out of my jeans and underwear, I fire it up and lie back on the bed. Spreading my folds, I slide a finger inside of me.

God, I'm already wet.

I push the vibrator inside, not wanting to waste a second. Immediate, sweeping relief floods my body.

The fingers on the top of the toy play with my clit as I push it in and out of me. I'm strung so tight, I'm ready to explode. It's been far too long since I've been with anyone. I joke about my players needing balance, but I have none.

Which leads me to getting off in a hotel in Miami. With Lydia's face flashing across my eyes.

It's her blue eyes I picture staring up at me. Her tongue I'm imagining flicking my clit. Her fingers pinching my nipples until I come. Her words encouraging me to ride her face to orgasm.

I push the vibrator in deeper, seeking relief.

"So good," I say to no one. "Let me come on your tongue."

"Delaney?"

It's like she's here in the room. Hearing her voice spurs me on.

I push one hand under my shirt to play with my nipples. Heat gathers in my core as I get closer and closer to release.

Just what I need.

A throat clears.

"Umm, Delaney?"

Oh shit.

Peeking one eye open, I see Lydia standing in the doorway to the bedroom.

"Fuck!" I shout, grabbing a pillow and trying to cover my exposed lower half as best I can. "What are you doing here?"

In a pair of cutoff shorts and a cropped tank top, water is dripping off of her.

"It started raining, so I thought I'd bring your jacket back." She holds up the black item in question. "I knocked and you didn't hear me. I thought you were gone, so I came in."

"Right."

Rain pelts the sliding glass door as a boom of thunder rolls through. It doesn't cover the vibrations of the toy still between my legs.

If there was ever a situation I didn't need her to walk in on, this was it.

"You can just put it on the dresser and leave." Embarrassment creeps up my cheeks. I want her out of my room as fast as possible. Whatever I was feeling before is gone.

She turns, looking behind her to throw it down, but doesn't make a move to leave. In fact, she takes a step closer to the bed.

"Why do I have to leave?"

"Because I want to die of embarrassment in peace."

"Or…"

Lydia takes another step closer.

"Or what?"

"Can I…" She licks her lips, eyes fluttering between the pillow that's covering my pussy and my face. "Can I help?"

"You…what?"

Lydia drops one knee on the bed. "You aren't the only one feeling something here."

"What are you talking about?"

A sheepish grin settles across her mouth. "I was checking your jacket pockets and—"

"Oh shit." If possible, my face goes even more red. "Look, I wasn't going to give it to you."

She shakes her head. "But I feel the same way. I have for a while now, D."

D.

It's the way she says it that has me throwing caution to the wind. Tossing the pillow to the side, I crook a finger at her.

"Then what are we waiting for?"

Lydia drops to the bed, crawling toward me. Her wet hair falls in waves around her as she moves up my half-naked body. Drops of water cool my overheated skin as her body settles on top of mine.

"Where do you want me to start?" She nips at my jaw.

I arch my hips up, cradling hers in mine.

"Finish what I started."

"Not yet."

Before I can argue, her mouth crashes against mine. My hands are greedy. Seeking out her skin where I can find it.

Her tongue demands entrance and I readily give it. Each soft stroke against mine amps up my pleasure. Butterflies are dancing in my stomach as I wrap my legs around her.

Warm lips trail a path down my body. Nipping and sucking on my skin.

"No more of this." Lydia grabs the still moving

vibrator and turns it off, chucking it toward my suitcase. "You're going to come on my tongue. Just how *I* like it."

There is nothing sexier than Lydia taking over. Thrusting my legs apart, she settles between them, but doesn't move any closer.

"I forgot just how much I loved your pussy." She drags a finger through the wet folds. "I could stay down here for hours and not get tired."

"Do it," I urge her on. "Please."

"Ooh, I like hearing you beg." She turns her lust-filled smile on me. "More."

"Please, Lydia. I've been dying to have your mouth on me since you walked into my locker room."

"More."

"God." I thrust a hand through my hair. "I forgot how much you make me crazy in the best way."

Her tongue darts out but only brushes my pussy.

"Ugh. That's just mean."

Lydia bites the tender skin on the inside of my thigh, kissing the sting away. She does the same to the other side. Repeating it, moving closer and closer to where I really want her.

By the time she sucks my clit into her mouth, I'm dripping.

"Gah!" Lust is pouring from me. I don't remember ever being wound so tight or having such a desperate desire for someone.

With each lick and suck, I'm a needy, wanton mess at Lydia's touch. Hungry for more.

"Are you going to come on my tongue?" she asks, blue eyes peering up at me.

"Yes. Make me."

Lydia pushes one finger inside of me, curling it as she blows warm air over my sensitive skin. It's the carnal lust licking through me that pushes me over the edge. That has me shouting her name.

"Lydia!"

Toe-curling waves of pleasure roll through me. It's the best I can remember feeling in a long time.

All at the hands of Lydia.

"That's it, baby. Ride it out," she purrs against my pussy.

"Oh God. So good. So damn good. Yes. Yesss."

I have no idea what I'm saying because I don't care. I don't care that I'm breaking every rule. All I care about is Lydia right now and how good she is making me feel.

By the time I'm floating back down to earth, Lydia's happy face is resting against my thigh.

"So, want to talk about a few things?"

Chapter Seventeen

LYDIA

When I came to Florida, I thought it'd be something new and fun to experience. My first major, national campaign for a swim company.

What I didn't plan on? Walking in on Delaney getting off.

Should I have turned around and left the room? Probably.

But standing there, seeing her in the throes of pleasure? I couldn't help myself.

I wanted Delaney more than anything in the moment and had to stay.

Licking her release off my lips, I rock back onto my heels. Kneeling between her spread legs, I can tell her entire body is blissed out. Diamond-hard nipples poke through the soft cotton of her T-shirt.

"What do you want to talk about?" she asks.

One hand is resting on her stomach and the other resting by her head.

"You. This. Us."

One eye peers up at me. "Or we can feel good right now and not worry about bigger things."

I smile down at her. "I don't mind that at all."

"Good." Delaney sits up, crossing her legs under her. "Did you finish your shoot?"

I shake my head, hopping off the bed to open the sliding glass door. It's warm in here now. My damp clothes are sticking to my overheated skin.

"Postponed until tomorrow morning."

"Does that mean you have the night off?" There's a hopeful note to Delaney's voice.

"Yeah. I do."

"Want to order room service?" she asks.

"That depends."

"On what?"

I move up the bed and drop down next to her, kicking my legs out across hers. "On if you're going to run out on me again."

Delaney threads her fingers through my hair. "Sorry, but I can promise that won't happen again."

"Why not?" I lean into her touch.

"Because I was struggling with my feelings for you. Not so much anymore."

"Good." I steal a kiss. "Because I don't think I'm struggling with my feelings anymore either."

Delaney grabs the menu and phones in our order. The cool breeze blows in as the two of us roll around in the sheets.

Languid kisses.

Searching hands.

Arching hips.

Delaney's weight above me is ratcheting up my need. But because a knock sounds on the door—one we both hear this time—nothing more can happen.

She slips on her underwear and fishes out a pair of shorts from her suitcase before answering the door and wheeling the tray into the bedroom.

"Always so good, Lyd," Delaney says, handing me my salad. She pulls a silver cover off a pepperoni pizza with a side of fries.

"Yours looks better."

"It will be. And if you're nice to me, then maybe I'll share a few fries."

Laughter bursts out of me. I feel lighter than I have in months. Who knew bringing this woman to her knees for me would make me feel like this?

"Well then, maybe I'll keep my questions light."

"Questions? What questions?" Delaney asks, dragging a fry through ketchup and stuffing it in her mouth.

"Like what you've been doing the last five years?"

The storm outside picks up. Sitting cross-legged on the bed next to Delaney, I stab a fork into my Cobb salad and take a bite.

"The exact same thing you've been doing." She laughs. "Hockey."

"I know that. You have to have been doing something else since I last saw you. The only thing I know is that you still like Dirty Shirleys and to draw on yourself."

"Technically, you were drawing on me." She smiles.

"Same difference."

"Really, hockey is all I've been doing."

I sigh. "Same. Do you think that's why we always got along so well?"

"Because we played hockey together once? No. You were easy to get along with and it was fun to be around you. I liked that. You always put everyone at ease. You still do. It's why you make a great captain."

I bite my lip to stop from beaming at her. "Thank you."

"It's true." She nudges my leg with her foot. "When I first saw you were on the team, I was worried about having to coach you, but you're the same old Lydia I remember."

"I hope some things have changed. I don't think I'm that same twenty-six-year-old from back then."

She shakes her head. "You're a better hockey player."

"And you're a coach now."

"Stating the obvious, Lyd."

"Hey, I wanted to know what you've been up to. That's new."

"What else do you want to know?" she asks.

"Let's do rapid-fire questions."

She groans. "Do we have to?"

"Yes. If you refuse to tell me what you've been doing these last five years besides hockey, I have to get this out of you somehow."

"Fine." Setting her plate down, she scoots closer to me. "Hit me."

"Travel by car or airplane?"

"Airplane. I like being able to multitask. I already know your answer."

I wince. "Again, having a healthy fear of planes is completely normal."

"Something that hasn't changed about you."

"Not at all." I shake my head. "You saw me when we hit turbulence."

"Do I need to assign you a plane buddy for away games when we travel?"

I nod. "You might have to. I wish it could be you."

"I'm sure Parker or Skylar will be there for you," she says.

"They would. Next question. What three things would you bring on a deserted island?"

Delaney points her finger in my face. "Okay, this one isn't fair."

"Why's that?" I tuck a stray lock of hair behind my ear as a gust of wind bursts into the room.

"Because you'll never get stuck on an island since you don't fly," she points out.

"Do you want me to go first then?"

She nods. "It seems only fair."

"Fine." I give her a playful smile. "If I could have three things on a deserted island, I'd bring—"

"Nothing hockey related. This has to be fun," Delaney interjects.

"I wasn't going to say hockey." I finish my last bite of salad and set it down on the tray next to the bed.

"Good. Continue."

"I was going to say my tablet, a knife, and maybe someone to enjoy it with."

"Doesn't that defeat the purpose of, you know, a *deserted* island?"

"Well, if my boat washes up on shore, I'd hope you'd be there with me to entertain me."

I can see her fighting the smile. "I'd be your entertainment?"

"Well." I return her smile. "In more ways than one."

"I see." She waggles her brows at me. "Then I guess, if our boat washes up on shore, I'll bring the vodka, a book, and the sunscreen. So we don't get burnt."

I burst out laughing. "You are so practical, D."

"Hey. If you're bringing me, that means I have three things to bring because you'll already be there."

"Fair."

"Here's a question for you," Delaney fires back. "Worst date you've ever been on?"

"Taking notes for our next date?"

"Curious, is all." She shrugs a shoulder. "I can't imagine you having a bad date."

"Oh no. I have had my fair share of bad dates. Men and women alike."

"Worst one then?"

"One of the girls on the team set me up with this guy whose family owned a funeral home. They were friends from childhood. Her husband was friends with him."

Her brown eyes go wide. "Oh God. I already don't think this is starting off well."

"Just wait. We go to dinner and I think it's going okay. He's cute and nice. But then once our dinner comes, I ask him about his work and he starts telling me how he makes people up when they die."

"He didn't!"

"Yes!" I shriek. "D, it was the wildest thing I'd ever heard. He asked me to go home with him and I couldn't get out of there fast enough."

"That just sounds like the start of a true crime podcast. Hockey player murdered after date with man wanting to make her up."

"You are not wrong." I burst out laughing. "Now, tell me your worst date."

"Please don't laugh," Delaney groans, burying her face in her hands.

"Why would I laugh?"

She rolls her eyes. "I don't even know if it would qualify as a date."

"Well, now you have to tell me."

"One of the professors at school tried to set me up with one of her friends. She wasn't big on first dates, so I thought if I planned something easy, it'd be good. Dinner downtown, maybe a movie after?"

"Sounds perfect to me," I tell her.

"I thought so too." She clears her throat, taking a sip of her drink. "I was waiting for her outside the restaurant when she pulled up. It was a small place in Burlington and there was only street parking. She tried parallel parking four times before she gave up and drove off. Left me standing there looking like an idiot."

"You're kidding."

She shakes her head. "Texted me after and said she believed since she couldn't park, that we weren't meant to be."

"Let me get this straight. So because she couldn't park, it was easier to leave?"

"Uh-huh." Delaney nods. "When I was standing right next to the valet."

I burst out laughing, tossing my head back. "Okay, you definitely win worst date."

Delaney holds what remains of her drink up in cheers. "I think you win."

I clink my water glass to hers. "Well, I might have missed out because last I heard the guy was married with two kids."

"To each their own." Delaney shakes her head. "I'm glad it didn't work out with him."

"Oh yeah?" I sip the rest of my water.

"Otherwise, I wouldn't be here with you."

"I guess that means you believe in second chances," I tell her.

"I wouldn't be here if *you* didn't believe in them."

"No, I guess not." Grabbing her legs, I pull her close to me.

Her skin is warm and soft. The easy smile on her face

has butterflies swarming low in my belly. I forgot how beautiful Delaney was. Maybe it was easier to forget so I wouldn't think about her every single day we were apart.

Because Delaney is not someone you forget. She's the kind of person that etches themselves into your soul, so deep that you think of them every day and the impact they had on your life.

I'm a better player because of her. She always pushed me. Ever the competitor, we were always striving to be the best. Hockey came naturally to me. But with Delaney on my line? We wanted to be at the top of our game.

"What are you thinking about?" she whispers, ghosting her fingers across my cheek.

Her touch is soft, but I feel it everywhere.

"You."

"Yeah?"

"How you're unforgettable."

Her gaze is tender. "I never forgot about you either, Lyd. How could I?"

Our lips crash together in need and desire. Passion and excitement. Frenzy and heat.

I don't know if I've ever been so hungry for someone. I can't get enough of this kiss. Of Delaney's taste. Of her tongue sliding against mine.

My hands roam over her body, pushing the thin T-shirt she's wearing up and over her head.

"I don't know if I'll ever have enough of you, Delaney."

"You already had me. I think it's time I have you."

Her words send heat sliding across my body. All I can thing about is this woman devouring every inch of me.

"Then have me."

Chapter Eighteen

LYDIA

"Stand up," Delaney commands. It sends shivers racking my body.

Dark brown eyes are locked on mine as I do as she asks. Standing on the side of the bed, Delaney follows suit. Her hands land on my hips and pull me close.

"Anything else you'd like me to do?" I drape my arms over her shoulders.

"Hmm." She presses a kiss just below my ear. "What do I want to do to you?"

Delaney steps out of my hold and circles me. A finger taps her chin. I'm ready to say fuck it and toss her down on the bed and have my way with her, but I don't.

Because I want to kneel before this woman. Have her do delicious things to my body that only she could do.

"Take off your shirt and shorts."

I waste no time pulling off my clothes. Her jaw drops as she takes me in. In nothing but a pair of underwear, I'm bare from the waist up.

Delaney drags a finger along the hem as she steps

behind me. Goose bumps explode over my skin at the soft touch.

"Gah!" A small gasp escapes.

"Do you like that?" Delaney's hand spreads across my stomach and pulls my back against her front. Heat ghosts my ear at her words.

"You know I do." Her hand drifts up farther, brushing the underside of my breasts. "Keep going."

"Funny. I didn't think you were the one in control here."

The loss of her touch is immediate.

"Is it a problem that I want more with you?" I cry out.

Delaney stands in front of me before peeling off her shirt and shorts. I bite down on my lip to keep from crying out again.

"Like what you see?"

"Yes. You look even sexier than I imagined."

"Have you been imagining me?" Delaney purrs.

"You know I have."

"What have you been imagining?" she asks, taking one step closer.

"You. Eating me out. Sitting on my face while I eat *you* out."

"I like the sound of that. Why don't we start with the first part?"

"Please." It comes out needier than I intended it to. But at this point, I don't care. I need Delaney's mouth on me. Anywhere. I'm not picky.

Putting one hand on my chest, she backs me up until I collide with the sliding glass door.

"Hands up. Keep them there."

"Yes."

"Good girl. That's the only word I want to hear out of your mouth."

"The only one?" I quirk a brow at her.

"Well, if you happen to shout my name as you come, I wouldn't be opposed to that."

"Good."

Delaney's hands tip my chin up as her mouth starts to trail a warm path down my jaw. My neck. My shoulder.

Whines and whimpers leave me as both her lips and hands explore my body. Every inch of my body is warm as she does delicious things to me.

Nibbles. Bites. Pinches.

I know by the time she pulls off my thong, it's going to be soaked through.

This is the feeling I loved experiencing with Delaney. No one ever knew my body like her. Knew how to tease and edge me before making me explode.

Only Delaney.

Her tongue darts out, licking between my abs. Her thumbs are playing with the satin material of my underwear.

My hips are arching into her touch.

"Patience, Lydia."

She pulls the material down and off, chucking it behind her. Delaney drags her nose down, kissing the bare mound above my clit.

"Leg up."

She pulls my thigh over her shoulder, leaving it there.

The sudden burst of air against my clit nearly sends me over the edge. Reciting hockey statistics is the only thing that prevents me from coming.

When I come, it's going to be on her tongue.

"Oh." I know she sees it. "When did you get this?"

I quirk a brow at her and she smiles.

"Yes, you can answer that," Delaney tells me.

"A few years ago."

She toys with the metal piercing in my clit.

"Why?"

Her gaze drops to my pussy. It's like she's mesmerized by it. I can't wait for her to play with it.

"What can I say? I can be hard to please and wanted to make it easier to get off."

"Funny." She smirks. "I never remember you being that way."

"You wrote the guide on how to please me," I confess.

"And now I get to add a new chapter."

Delaney seals her mouth over my clit and pulls on the metal piercing.

"Holy fuck!" I can't help it.

Because…holy fuck.

One swipe of her tongue against my sensitive flesh and I could combust. The way she plays with my piercing? I should have known Delaney would have no problem with it.

As her tongue expertly plays with my clit, she slides two fingers inside me.

"I forgot how good you taste, Lyd. So sweet. So fucking good I could live off the taste of you alone."

"Do it."

I urge her on, not caring I'm ignoring her directions. I feel her smile against my wet folds as she curls her fingers against the walls of my pussy.

"Your body, Lydia. You're the sexiest damn person on the planet."

Heat sizzles in my veins at her words. Tension slides down my spine. I'm ready to fucking explode when she rocks back onto her heels.

Two fingers are still moving inside me as I watch her free hand disappear into her underwear that she still has on.

"Can't help yourself?"

She grins at me before sucking my clit back into her mouth. Everything else is forgotten as I dig my heel into her back to urge her on.

Her fingers and mouth work together.

Harder. Faster.

"Delaney! Yes! Oh God, yes!"

My hands search for purchase on the glass window, needing to hold on for dear life as I fly off to the stratosphere.

Toe curling, fireworks, fire. I feel all of it at Delaney's touch.

"Holy shit, D. I think I blacked out."

Sitting back, she's wiping her mouth. Her eyes are wide, filled with lust. And she said I was the sexiest person on the planet? She clearly didn't take herself into account.

Delaney grabs my hand and pulls us both toward the bed. We collapse in a post-sex haze, bodies intertwined. Hands are groping as lips are searching.

The two of us are blissed out and sated. Two incredible orgasms will do that to you. It's the perfect feeling.

"So…"

"So what?" she asks, dragging her fingers along my scalp.

"Was this a one-time thing?"

"Do you want it to be?" she fires back.

"No. Do you?"

"No, I don't either." She pauses, shifting so we're now facing each other. "But what about the team? We can't be together."

Grabbing her around the waist, I pull her closer to me.

"As long as no one finds out…"

"You're okay breaking the rules?"

"You're the rule follower." I kiss the tip of her nose.

"You make me want to throw the rule book out the window."

This time, I move her under me and lie on top of her.

"Then I guess we should break some more rules tonight."

Chapter Nineteen

My arms are filled to the brim with bags. Trying to shoulder open the door into my house when my phone starts buzzing requires the skill of a juggler.

Hoping it's not Lydia calling to cancel—which would be the sensible thing to do since we shouldn't be doing this—I breathe a sigh of relief when I see who it is.

"Hey, Mom." I unlock the door and drop the bags on the floor. "How are you?"

"Oh, you know. Just calling because my only offspring doesn't feel the need to call me and keep me updated on her life."

I snort a laugh as I grab two bags and carry them into the kitchen. "Mom. I called you a few days ago."

"And a few days ago you didn't have the biggest win of your life."

I roll my eyes, setting the bags on the counter and starting to unload everything I got for dinner.

"You texted me after the game. I texted you back."

"And? That kind of win deserves a phone call."

I laugh. "Then call me next time."

"I'm calling you now."

"You are." I grab the container of sushi I picked up from the restaurant and put it in the refrigerator. With Lydia not coming over for another hour, the last thing I want is lukewarm sushi to make either of us sick. "How's everything at home?"

"Did I tell you that Marcy's son is getting divorced?"

"He is?" That draws me up short. "I thought he and his husband were madly in love."

"Oh no. It was quite the scandal. You should hear what everyone is saying about it. Not very nice things about how it brings shame to the sacred institution of marriage."

"Do you know what happened?"

"I don't. But Marcy will be at knitting club tomorrow night, so I'll be sure to get the scoop."

I can only imagine what her small town is saying if Marcy's son is getting divorced. It's not the most welcoming of places. It was one of the reasons I was so keen to leave.

"How's knitting club going?" It is one of her many new hobbies since she decided to retire.

"You know how those things are. It's more gossip than anything. They do love hearing about you and the team."

I smile through the phone. "Well, hopefully I'm doing them proud."

"Who cares about them? You're making me proud."

"Thanks, Mom. Listen, I can't talk right now. I have a date tonight."

"Ohh." I can hear her excitement through the phone. "Who's the lucky man?"

I swallow back the disappointment swimming through me at her words. I hate that I'm lying to her. But based on how scandalous people think Marcy's son's divorce is, it's why I'm hesitant to come out to her.

"I'll be sure to tell you more if something comes of it."

"Always so quiet on the dating front," she chides. "You have fun and I'll be sure to call you next week."

"Not if I call you first."

"That's my girl. I love you, Delaney."

"Love you, Mom."

I hang up and drop my phone onto the island, pressing the heels of my hands into my eyes.

This is not what I wanted before my first date with Lydia. Worrying about my mom and how she'll react when I tell her I'm a lesbian. Well, when I *eventually* tell her.

Maybe.

Hopefully.

Needing to clear my head, I start bustling around the kitchen to make sure that everything is in order for our date tonight.

Outside of hockey, one of my other passions is home decorating. If there's a home reno show, I've watched it.

Digging the place mats and the candles out of the drawer, I set the dining room table. Does it look weird to only have two places set on a table made for eight? Yes. But I don't care.

Because Lydia is coming over. For a first date.

It's not like I need to impress her. I think shared orgasms in Miami got the point across fairly well.

It's been a few weeks since we got home. Between games starting again and the holidays, we didn't have much time to get together.

Read: any.

She took a quick two-day trip to visit her brother and his new baby, while I had my mom up to visit. In all that time, I'm surprised I didn't talk myself out of this thing with her. While I don't want to do anything to jeopardize my position with the team, it's Lydia.

The one that got away.

And being with her tonight is all I want.

I shift the gold silverware around until I get it exactly where I want it on top of the black-and-white striped placemat.

Knowing Lydia doesn't drink during the season, I bypass the wine glass and make myself my own Dirty Shirley cocktail while I get everything else ready. It helps to soothe my nerves.

Why am I so nervous?

Is it because I'm her coach and she's my player? That if this goes sideways, then it's going to be awkward every day at practice?

Or because I know what she used to mean to me, and I want it to be more?

This is why I never really dated. Hockey is easy. Give me a puck and a stick and I can teach anyone how to play. Feelings? I don't know what to do with them.

Taking the edamame out, I snack on a few pieces as I put the finishing touches on the table. Just because we can't go out, doesn't mean we can't have the first-date experience here.

Looking at the time, it's still about twenty minutes until she gets here. But knowing her, she'll arrive early.

Everything looks perfect. Striking a match, I light the candles and grab my drink to head into the living room. I light my favorite candle. The pine smell is something I love having any time of the year.

Before I can sit down, the doorbell rings. I take one last calming deep breath to settle my nerves.

Through the tempered glass of the front door, I see Lydia standing there. How can someone look that sexy through a door?

Only Lydia could do it.

Lydia greets me with a smile as I swing open the door. I drink her in.

Tight black jeans. Oversized pink sweater that hangs off one shoulder. Gold hoops in her ears.

"Are you just going to stand there all night, or are you going to let me in?"

My gaze snaps to hers. A playful look sits on her face.

"Sorry." I sweep my arm out, welcoming her in, giving her an impish smile.

"Wow. This is a great place, D."

D.

It causes my insides to swirl as I watch her spin around, taking everything in.

"Thanks."

She beams back at me when her blue eyes lock on to mine. "It reminds me of your old place."

"Are you calling me a creature of habit?"

"I think we've established the two of us are creatures of habit."

Passing by her on the way to the kitchen, I give her a quick peck on the cheek as I pass.

She stops me with a warm hand to the arm. "What, that's all I get?"

"Don't dates usually end in kisses?"

She shrugs a slim shoulder, her sweater slipping farther down.

"Well, how about we change it up and start the date with a kiss?"

"That seems like sound logic," I tell her.

Lydia rests a hand on my hip and pulls me close. Even through the black cotton of my plain, long-sleeved black shirt—dressed up with my favorite necklace, a pair of crossed hockey sticks—I feel her heat.

Her eyes flit down to my lips as her teeth bury into her plump bottom lip.

Brushing her hair off her shoulder, I press a kiss to the exposed skin.

A shudder racks her body. I love that this is the reaction I bring out in her. I thought what we had in Miami was going to be a one and done thing. Fuck around for the night and get it out of our systems.

But as Lydia's nails dig into my side, I know it's more. Her body is reacting to mine the same way I'm reacting to hers.

With sheer need and desire.

I place soft kisses up her neck. Vanilla overwhelms my senses as I suck and nibble my way over her tender skin.

"Stop teasing me."

"I thought you wanted me to kiss you?" I whisper, tugging her earlobe between my teeth.

"Yes. On the mouth."

I pull back, looking her in the eye. "Thank you for clarifying."

As I rub my thumb back and forth across her bottom lip, she sucks it into her mouth, swirling her tongue around it. A needy moan escapes me.

"See? Not so fun, is it?"

When Lydia releases my digit, I crush my lips to hers. Heat and electricity ignite around us as our tongues tangle, fighting for control.

It's the most delicious kiss I've had in a long time. The give and take of it. Her fingers sliding into my hair. My hands pulling her closer.

I swallow every gasp and moan as our moves become less hurried. More languid and casual. Like we're relearning each other's mouths again.

"Mmm." Lydia smiles against my lips. "I love that you taste like cherries."

"And you still smell like a cupcake."

Lydia nips at my lips one more time before stepping back. "I think we really should start each date like this."

"I'll try."

Linking our fingers together, I pull her after me toward the kitchen.

"Or we could just take this date right upstairs."

Spinning on my heel, I shake my head at her. "No way. I have quite the meal planned for you. Now, go sit and I'll bring it over."

Lydia steals a kiss before walking over to the table. "This is quite the treatment, D."

"What can I say? You know it's my love language."

I pull out the platter of sushi and the sides and carry them over to the table. Heading back, I top off my drink and grab one of the sparkling waters I know Lydia likes.

"You still remembered my favorite?" she asks, taking the can from me.

"Shot in the dark." I wink.

"This looks great, Delaney. You didn't have to go to all this trouble."

Taking the seat across from her, I hold my drink up to clink against hers. "I did. It's our first date."

"We've gone on dates before," Lydia tells me, helping herself to a little bit of everything.

"Have we? Because I'm pretty sure we only hit bars after games when we played together."

Using the chopsticks, I grab a salmon roll, dunking it into the soy sauce and eating it.

Lydia points her own chopstick at me. "Okay, maybe not."

"See?" I shrug. "I had to pull out all the stops."

"You could have ordered in pizza and I would have been happy," Lydia tells me.

"Good to know."

Even though we're sitting at my dining room table, it has all the feel of a first date. Rediscovering one another. Flirting. Coy smiles.

Being with Lydia is everything I remember it to be. Only better somehow. We're older, more settled.

"Do you have any more pictures of Cameron?" I ask, biting into my last salmon roll.

"Do I ever." Her face glows as she stands, walking around the table and sitting on my lap. "Look how freaking cute she is."

Lydia wraps her arm around my shoulders as I rest my hands on her hips. She opens the photo app on her phone and starts swiping through all the photos of her new niece.

"Oh my God." I swipe back to the one of her in a tiny Rosebuds jersey. "This is the cutest thing I've ever seen."

"Right? I don't have one with her and the stuffed hockey stick, but it was precious."

"She is already so spoiled by you."

"Not just me. Everyone. I can't wait until I get to visit longer."

"Do you ever regret being so far away from your family?" I ask.

"Never. Hockey is worth it." She shakes her head, glancing at her watch. "Which makes this even harder to leave because I want to stay all night."

"I know." I squeeze her hips as she stands, starting to clear the table before heading to the door.

"If only we didn't have an early morning practice. Our coach works us too hard."

"I appreciate your coach's dedication to the team." I smile at her. "As your girlfriend, I hate it."

Laughter bubbles out of her. "I'm your girlfriend now? Have we discussed this?"

I shrug a shoulder. "I only assumed."

"Assume away. As long as it means my little rule follower is okay breaking the rules for me."

"Only for you, Lydia."

"Good. Now, I have a dog waiting for me at home."

"Next time bring him over so you can stay later."

She grins at me. "I will."

Because now that I've had Lydia in my space, I don't want her to leave.

Ever.

Chapter Twenty

LYDIA

"Hey, Dad. It's me. Lydia. Just wanted to check in and see how things were going. I know you're in New York and Boston a lot for work and we've got a few games there coming up. If you're around, I was thinking we could get together for dinner. Give me a call. Bye."

I hang up the call, pacing in front of the small salon as I wait for Skylar. She's twenty minutes late, something very unlike her. I figured it'd be a good time to try and call my dad.

We start the week with a home game against Ottawa before leaving on a short road trip to Boston and New York. I'm hoping if he's in New York, I might be able to have dinner with him after our afternoon game.

If only he would answer my calls. Or emails.

After practice this morning, I was feeling good so I figured I'd try.

No good.

I glance down the sidewalk and see Skylar running in my direction. Everything about her demeanor raises the hairs on my arm.

"What's wrong?"

"Brian dumped me." She throws herself into my arms, sobbing on my shoulder.

"What? What happened?" I asked. "I thought things were going well? I thought it was all okay over the holidays? Weren't you looking at engagement rings?"

Skylar swipes an angry tear away as we walk inside. "He said he doesn't like living in Toronto. Being away from friends and family was too hard on him. I think he was fine over the holidays because we were both home."

"Oh, babe. I'm so sorry."

One of the technicians shows us to our usual chairs. This has become our thing together. A way to spoil ourselves during the season every few weeks. She hands us the colors as they start running a warm bath of water.

"I thought he knew what he was getting into?" I reach over and grab her hand, giving it a squeeze.

"I thought so too. Apparently not."

"I'm so sorry, Skylar. Can I do anything to help?"

She looks over at me, eyes red-rimmed and tears spilling over her cheeks. "Maybe we can have a girls' night tonight? You, me, and Parker?"

"Yes. We'll binge all the snack foods and watch trashy TV at my place."

"That sounds great."

"Just try to relax right now and I'll text Parker and let her know."

She gives my hand a squeeze before relaxing back into the chair. "Thank you. You're a great friend."

"Anything."

Pulling out my phone, I let the chair massage my back as I start texting two different people.

LYDIA

Brian broke up with Skylar

Girls night at my place tonight

PARKER

That asshole!

Let me know what I can bring

You bring the drinks, I'll get the snacks

Perfect

PULLING UP ANOTHER TEXT, I fire off a message to Delaney.

LYDIA

I can't come over after all

DELANEY

Got a hot date? 😉

Not quite

Skylar's boyfriend broke up with her

That hurts. I'm sorry

How's she doing?

Heartbroken

Take care of her

I'll see you another night

Maybe after our game tomorrow?

Yes

Do you want to take longer to think about it?

Don't need to

I want to see you

Bring Biscuit

I see what this is about

You just want to hang out with my dog

I thought that was obvious

And here I thought you liked me

Kind of

Oh good

Just kind of

A lot

Good

Because I kind of like you a lot too

I LOCK my phone and close my eyes. I don't need Skylar to see how happy I am. Not when she's devastated from Brian leaving her. I hate that she's heartbroken while I'm happier than I've ever been. Even if time with Delaney is few and far between, I take any chance I can get with her.

And after our next game? I'm not going to let anything come between us.

.X.

"THAT ASSHOLE!" It's the first thing out of Parker's mouth when she walks into my apartment. "Does he think he can do better than our Skylar? Fuck, no."

"Hi to you too."

"Hi." She pecks me on the cheek as I follow her into the kitchen. "I can't believe this happened."

"I know."

"It makes me glad I'm single."

"God, me too," I say.

The lie slips out too easily. I want to tell them about Delaney. About the woman they don't get to see on the ice. But until we can figure out how to have a future together, I stay quiet about my present.

The buzzer rings through the apartment and I go to let Skylar in. When she gets off the elevator, she looks a touch more put together than she did this afternoon.

"Sky. I am so sorry." Parker sweeps her into a hug.

"Thanks, Parker." Her lip quivers as she squeezes Parker tight.

"C'mon. I have all sorts of snacks."

"Are you going to binge them with me?"

I smile at her, wrapping an arm around her shoulders and leading her into the living room. "Yes. I made mac and cheese for dinner and have buffalo dip, guacamole, and gummy bears."

"That sounds amazing."

It's all laid out on the counter, Biscuit keeping a watchful eye.

"And maybe Biscuit can give you some extra snuggles," I say.

"I'd love that." Skylar scoops him up into her arms as he peppers her face with kisses.

"Want me to get you something?"

"Gummy bears, please. I'm easy."

Parker chucks the bag onto the couch and helps herself to a little of everything. I do the same and grab a beer. The only one I'll have tonight. Parker takes the empty seat next to Skylar and hands her a drink before I drop down onto the floor.

Biscuit hops out of Skylar's arms and comes to sit next to me, eyes firmly fixed to my plate.

"None for you. I'll get you a bone later." I kiss his cheek.

"Maybe I need a dog now," Skylar cries. "No one else is going to love me."

"You'll find someone. You're too amazing to not find someone," Parker says. "You're one of my favorite people, besides Lydia."

"Aww. Here's to us." We clink our bottles together.

"Thanks, ladies. I don't know what I would do if I didn't have you." Skylar sniffs. "Breakups suck."

"Whatever you need, we're here for you," I say.

"What Lydia said. If you want to binge terrible movies every night for the next two weeks, we're here for you."

"Or bash him. We can do that too," I tell her. "Or if you just want to cry, we've each got shoulders for you."

Skylar pops open the bag of gummy bears and tears the head off of one. "This is all I need for now. And maybe more Biscuit snuggles."

Biscuit's attention snaps to her at the sound of his name. He goes to her in search of scraps that he doesn't get. Only snuggles.

"You're welcome anytime. He won't say no."

"Truffle is at your disposal too," Parker says.

"I'm glad you two both have emotional support dogs for me." Skylar gives us a sad smile.

"Why don't we put on a movie?" Parker suggests.

"As long as it's not a rom-com. I can't handle love right now."

Grabbing the remote, I pass it over to Skylar to pick a movie. To no one's surprise, she picks a thriller. Nothing I would normally watch, but I'll suffer through it for her.

Skylar and Parker get cozy on the couch with Biscuit between them and I lean against their legs. If I couldn't spend the night with Delaney, I'm glad I'm with these two.

It's hard not being near family, but having these ladies around makes it feel like we have our own tight-knit circle.

It also makes me thankful for what I have with Delaney. Pulling out my phone, I sneak a glance at my friends. Their focus is on the movie. I type a quick text out.

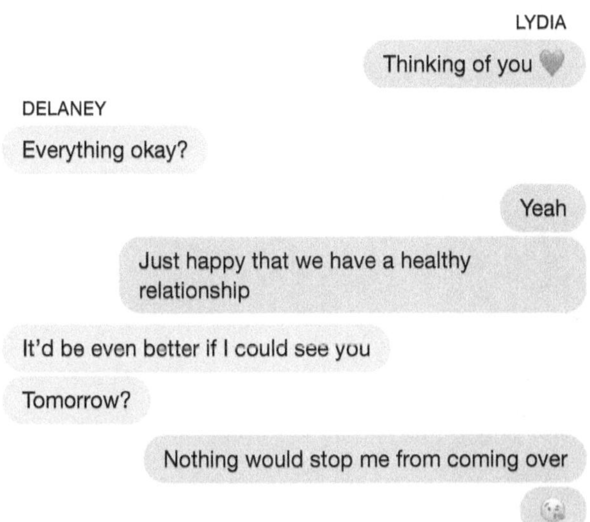

Good

See you after the game

I can't wait

"ARE YOU PAYING ATTENTION?" Parker asks.

"Sorry." I lock my phone and set it on the coffee table.

At least I can think of Delaney while watching this movie.

"Are you good?" Skylar asks.

"What more could I need? I have you three."

"Three?" Parker questions.

"Three." I grab Biscuit and bury my face in his soft fur. "Biscuit counts."

But I leave off the most important person.

Because as long as I have these three—and Delaney—I have everything I need.

Chapter Twenty-One

DELANEY

"We still have another period of hockey to play, ladies. We're only down by two goals. Plenty of time to clean things up and put another couple of goals on the board."

I look around at the team. Heads are hanging and we look beaten. Ottawa brought their A game tonight.

Clean stickhandling. Passes. Shots on goal. Everything has been on point.

While we've been chasing them all night. No matter what we seem to be doing, we can't catch up. Both Lydia and Skylar have had some incredible shots on goal, but to no avail. It's like their goalie's glove is a magnet to the puck.

"We've got this," Lydia chimes in from her spot on the bench. "Work together as a team and the game is in the bag."

It helps to pump up the team, but by the time we're back out on the ice, our energy is flagging. We've played from behind, but it hasn't felt like this. Like we can't come back.

When Ottawa gets an early goal in the third period, and we're down by three, the mood shifts to hopeless. A collective moan issues from the home crowd, as people start to leave.

"I think we should switch up the lines. See if mixing it up might help," I tell Bailey.

She nods at my command and marches down the bench to start letting the women know when they'll be hitting the ice. But before we can do much of anything, Ottawa gets another goal.

"Damn it," I swear under my breath. "Bailey, go ahead and change it up now."

"Got it, Coach."

She nods, calling those on the ice back to the bench and sending others out. Lydia and Skylar take their seats and are discussing the game as play resumes.

5-1.

While not impossible to come back from, it's not feeling like it's going to happen.

"Okay, tighten up, ladies. Let's get some of these goals back." I walk up and down the bench, hyping the girls up. "Play your game. Rely on your training. No mistakes."

Lydia flies off the bench and I watch her go.

"C'mon. C'mon."

She's flying down the ice with only one defender in front of her.

"Let's go, Bishop!" someone shouts from the bench.

The crowd is urging her on as she crosses into our attacking zone. With quick stick work, she dekes out the goalie and gets it into the back of the net.

"Yes!"

Enthusiastic cheers ring out through the arena. Not the most excited our crowd has ever been, but it's hard when we're still down by three.

With only five minutes left, it's going to be hard to tie it up. Especially with the way Ottawa has been playing tonight.

Parker is able to hold off Ottawa's advances, and with two minutes left, I pull her from the game in favor of another winger on the ice.

We're surging, but every shot on goal is blocked.

By the time the final horn sounds, the score is 5-2.

I shove an angry hand through my hair. It was not our night. We didn't play our best and Ottawa outshone us on every level.

It's the answers I give the awaiting press as I head back down the tunnel after congratulating our opponent on their win.

The sight that greets me in the locker room is hanging heads and dejection. I hate it. There is nothing worse than losing. We've been on a hot streak, so it makes it sting even more.

"Listen up," I call out, but it's not needed since no one is talking. "Losing isn't fun. It never is. But we're going to learn from this. Study what didn't go right, and put it into action so we can improve upon it for our next game."

"Yes, Coach," a few voices ring out.

"Get cleaned up and get a good night's sleep. I'll see you all here bright and early tomorrow for practice."

A few of the women smile back at me, but there's not much behind it.

Heading to my office, I sink down into my chair and let out a heavy sigh.

Fuck. I hate losing. I really do. I don't know any person that likes to lose.

I'm tempted to pick up my tablet to watch highlights of the game. But I don't need to do that. I need to separate myself from the game for at least a few hours.

"You need anything before we head out?" Nadia peeks her head into my office.

"No, I'm good. I'll see you tomorrow."

"Bailey told me to tell you not to worry too much. It's one game and she says not to spend all night studying film."

I smile at her. "Should I be concerned with how well she knows me?"

"No, because we know you and know exactly what you're going to go home and do."

"Hey." I point a finger at her. "I was debating if I wanted to start now."

"Of course." Nadia waves goodbye and shuts the door behind her.

I rest my head against the back of the chair and close my eyes. Even though I'm not watching film, I'm already thinking of everything that we need to clean up.

Passes weren't great tonight. We'll need to work on that. Our defenders weren't where they needed to be, leaving Parker open. Nadia will need to help them tomorrow.

I can't help thinking about all of this. My brain never wants to shut off.

A soft knock comes from the door.

"I promise, Nadia, I'm not watching film."

"You're not?"

"Lydia?" Opening my eyes, there she is, looking more tired than I've ever seen her. "What are you still doing here?"

She walks into my office, leaving the door open behind her. At least if we're not the only ones still here, no one can accuse us of fraternizing. "You're the last one here so I just wanted to make sure you're okay before I left."

That answers that question.

I peer behind her, dropping my voice. "Aren't you coming over tonight?"

She smiles, nodding at me. "Yeah. But just wanted to check on you."

"Are you okay? It was a tough game tonight."

"Sore, but I'll live. Nothing a little time in the ice bath won't cure."

"Good." I stand, locking my tablet in the drawer. Film really can wait until tomorrow. "Want to head out?"

"I thought you'd never ask." Lydia steps back as I lock my office. "I just need to grab Biscuit."

"I can't wait to see him."

"And me?" she whispers, grinning at me.

"I'm seeing you now."

"Not how you'd really like." Lydia winks.

"Then hurry your ass up."

Because I can't wait to be with Lydia again.

Chapter Twenty-Two

DELANEY

"Hey, Mom."

"Hi, sweetheart. Tough loss tonight."

"I know." I kick my feet up on the coffee table, watching a light snow start to fall. "Wasn't our best game."

"You'll bounce back. I know you will."

I smile, even though she can't see me. "We'll need to work on cleaning things up."

"Don't worry about that until tomorrow. I know, I know. I can feel you rolling your eyes at me."

"Hey. There was no rolling of the eyes," I fire back. Only because she called me out before I could do it.

"When's your next game?"

"We've got a couple of days here before we're on the road to Boston and New York."

"Ohh, Boston." Mom's voice kicks up a notch. "They've been on a hot streak."

"Do you watch all the games?" I ask.

"Not all of them. Just some."

"Well, Lydia used to play for them, so I'm sure she can help us during practice to get ready."

"Oh, that's right. Make sure Lydia gives you the inside scoop on them so you can beat them."

It's weird to hear my mom say her name so casually in conversation. She has no idea what she means to me. All because I'm too scared to tell her when all I want to do is be able to share it with her.

I've always imagined having this talk with her. Of sitting down in her living room and telling her over a glass of wine. But now, with a sudden need to tell her, I question if doing so over the phone is really the right time.

I don't want to lose this courage, so I start, "Mom, I umm…"

"Oh, sorry, Delaney. I need to go. The girls are here for book club."

"Oh, okay."

"Did you need to tell me something?"

"It can wait until later. Go, have fun with your wine club." I give a halfhearted laugh.

"You know me so well, dear." She laughs back. "Love you."

"Love you too."

So much for telling her. Maybe that was a sign this isn't a conversation you do over the phone. Ugh. I hate that I can't do it.

"Knock, knock."

Using the code to the front door, Lydia lets herself in. A tiny blur of fur comes flying in. It pushes the nervous feelings aside.

Because who can be upset with a puppy charging at you?

"There's my favorite guy."

Biscuit comes bursting into the living room, running straight to me. He attacks my face with kisses and nips on my ear.

"What have I said about trying to eat people?" Lydia laughs, scooping him up into her arms. "We can kiss people, but no trying to chew off their ears, okay?"

He answers her with a nip to the chin.

"He doesn't like listening, does he?"

"We're working on it. Sit and stay is where we're at right now."

"Do you want to try something else?"

"Like what?" Lydia asks, setting Biscuit down, who runs to the couch and leaps on it.

"Maybe shake? I've been doing some research."

"Research. On training dogs." It comes out as a statement.

"Is that okay?"

A smile slides over her mouth as she pulls me close. "You looked into how to train my dog. I love it and how much you love him."

"Well, if he's going to be over here with you, I figured it'd be a good thing to do."

Giving me a quick kiss, Lydia releases me. "C'mere, Biscuit."

His head perks up before giving us a yawn and lying back down.

"I don't think he wants to do this either."

"Biscuit. Come." There's more of a command this time in her voice and he obeys. "Good boy."

She rubs behind his ears as I go to the kitchen to grab my box of treats.

"Here you go." I give him the treat as he keeps searching for more. "Okay. Let's try shake."

I say the word as I put his paw in my hand. We do this for a few times before I have Lydia do it.

"Can you shake, Biscuit?" she asks.

He studies her before waving his paw in front of her.

"Hey. That's good for a first try," I tell her.

"It's because my dog is the smartest dog in the world."

I snort laugh. "Of course you think that."

"Are you saying this isn't the face of the smartest dog in the world?"

She squishes his face and it does funny things to my heart to see the two of them together.

This thing between the two of us is still new and fresh. At least, it feels that way even with our history.

Even though we have to pretend at the rink that nothing is going on between us, I can't deny the pull.

We fell back into this so easily, and being with her here now is just what I need.

"Hey."

"What?" she asks, as I pull her close.

"I'm glad you're here." I give her a soft smile.

"I am too."

Biscuit jumps up, pawing at both of our legs.

"Does that mean he needs to go outside?" I ask.

"Yes." Lydia nods. "Want to make out while he does his business?"

"Hell, yes."

We let him out the back door before I push Lydia down onto one of the barstools.

Her lips are wet, eyes focused on my own mouth. I step between her legs and brush the hair off her shoulder. The vein in her neck throbs with need.

I love seeing what I do to Lydia.

This woman is incredible. The person I want most in the world.

I tug her bottom lip between my teeth. I swallow her gasp as I thread my fingers through her hair. The soft locks tangle as I tip her head back to explore her mouth.

Soft and sweet.

Heated and hurried.

I change my pace as we make out like teenagers in the kitchen.

Her fingers play with the hem of my sweatshirt as she pulls me closer. I can see this being our life. The two of us going to hockey practice or games. Coming home to Biscuit. Having kids.

I shouldn't be thinking so far ahead with Lydia, but I can't help it.

When it comes to Lydia Bishop, I want it all.

Chapter Twenty-Three

LYDIA

P ure happiness is oozing from Delaney. It's infectious.

Sitting here, making out with her, is everything I need after a tough loss. Hell, being with her any time of the day is exactly what I need.

Delaney Charles is everything I want.

And right now, I need to make the two of us forget what happened tonight.

"Want to take this upstairs?"

Her nose brushes against mine as she nods. "Let's put Biscuit in his kennel."

"I love that you got one for him."

"Well, if I want you to stay, then we needed it."

It makes my heart clang around in my chest at the thought of how caring Delaney is. It's a simple thing—a crate for my dog. But it means a lot more.

That this thing between the two of us is serious.

Calling him inside, I grab the box of treats and lead him to the crate with a towel lining it. He happily crunches on his treat before curling into a tight circle.

"Good boy."

I grab Delaney's hand and pull her up to her room. It's been far too long since I've had her. Since that night tucked away in the hotel room in Miami. I love that the two of us put hockey first, and while we've had a few make-out sessions, I need more.

Crave more.

I'm hungry. Hungry for Delaney. For her luscious body. For her mouth. Her pussy. I want every inch of this woman.

Pulling Delaney into the room, I push her up against the wall and kick the door shut.

"I can't wait to taste you again. Fucking feral for it." I arch my hips into hers. "Want to lap up every drop of your orgasm."

"Yesss," she hisses. "Do it. Please."

I drop to my knees, undoing the button and zipper on her black pants. Before I can get any farther, Delaney grabs my hand.

"Wait. Stop."

"What's wrong? Did you change your mind?"

"Umm, no."

Delaney holds my hand against the soft material of her pants, not letting me move. "That doesn't sound convincing."

"Oh God. I'm so embarrassed." She slaps her free hand over her face.

"What's wrong?" I ask, rocking back onto my heels.

"I…uhh, God. I forgot to, you know…shave. Down there."

"That's what you're worried about?"

"I honestly forgot you were coming over tonight. I meant to take care of it before, but I got distracted."

"Distracted?" I ask, quirking a brow at her. "What do you mean?"

"I, umm…" she falters.

"Tell me."

"I was going to do it but then you sent me the photos from your shoot."

"And?"

"And I got distracted and had to get off."

"Really?"

"Ugh, yes." She drops a hand onto my shoulder. "You were so fucking sexy that I had to do it immediately."

"I like hearing that. How much I turn you on."

"You know you do."

"Well then." I pull her hand away from mine and finger the soft material of her pants. "Would you like to take care of that problem?"

"You mean…"

"I'll do it. Let me."

"You would do that? You'd *want* to?"

I stand back up, resting both hands on either side of her head. "Yes. I want to. Now, stop stalling and come with me because it means I get to eat that delicious pussy of yours."

I lead Delaney to the bathroom and watch as she flips on the shower, turning the water to hot.

Delaney leans against the glass door. "I guess that means you're in charge tonight?"

"Yes. Now, strip."

As she takes off her clothes, I do the same. It's hard not to drool over her naked body as it's revealed to me.

Delaney Charles is the sexiest woman I know, and I love that I get her like this.

Dropping my thong into the pile, I grab her by the hips and push her into the shower. Steam swirls around us as I press my lips to hers. Water streams down our bodies as our hands grope over one another.

"Where's your razor?" I whisper.

"On the bench seat."

Peering behind me, I see it and the shaving cream. Grabbing both, I turn back to Delaney with a cunning grin on my face as I drop to my knees.

I take her ankle in my hand and rest it on the bench next to me. Her back is to the water, casting mist around me. I pop off the cap to the bottle and spray a foaming bubble in my hand.

As I spread the cream along her pussy, she tosses her head back on a moan. "It shouldn't feel this good."

I nip at the inside of her thigh. "Just wait."

Rinsing my hands in the water, I grab the razor and kiss my way back up her leg. Her skin is warm. Soft. Everything I love as I tease her. When I get to the apex of her thighs, I take a beat. I'm so turned on by this that I need a minute to breathe.

It's intimate in a way I've never experienced. Doing this with Delaney is right. She's the only person I would want to do this with.

Locking eyes with her, I wink at her before affixing my attention to the matter at hand.

Starting at the top, I drag the razor down her skin. A groan slips out as I rinse the head off. As I move across her pussy, her hands sink into my wet hair. I punctuate each swipe with a kiss to her thigh. I'm careful around her soft folds, already glistening with need.

"Holy shit, Lyd. I'm going to come."

"Not yet. I'm almost done."

A sob escapes this time. "Hurry. Please."

"I am going to take my time. I have all night to do whatever I want with you."

I reverse my motions, swiping up this time. The only

thing I don't do is nip and suck on her thigh. I know it's driving her crazy by the way her hands fist in my hair.

I touch her everywhere but where she really wants me.

When I'm done, I kiss just below her belly button and stand.

"Time to inspect my work."

"What are you doing?"

Reaching behind her, I grab the showerhead and pull it off the base. Kneeling before her, I run it over her soft skin. As I do, I sink a finger inside her.

"Oh God, Lydia!" Delaney throws her hands against the wall, holding on as I attack her clit with the shower-head. "That feels incredible."

Pulling the head back, I suck the tiny, throbbing ball of nerves into my mouth and flick my tongue over it. Muttered cries bounce around in the enclosed space as I go back and forth between my mouth and the nozzle. I scissor two fingers in and out of her as I watch pleasure course over her body.

I have never seen Delaney look more wanton. It's the kind of thing wet dreams are made of. But only for me.

No one else will ever get this.

Dropping the showerhead to the floor, I pull my fingers out of her and slide my tongue into her. Pinching and squeezing her clit sends her over the edge.

"Yes, baby. Come on my tongue for me."

"Yes! Fuck!"

I lap up every drop of her release as the air starts to cool around us. The hard floor beneath me digs into my knees. But I don't care.

Not as long as I have this woman at my mercy.

I hold her up as she comes down from her orgasm. When she looks down at me, it's with a sated look on her face.

"Come here."

She wiggles a finger at me and I stand. Threading her fingers through my hair, she pulls me in for a languid kiss.

Our tongues lazily chase one another as we stand in the quickly cooling shower. I could stay here forever. It's the perfect ending to a crappy day.

"Mmm. D. That was incredible," I say.

"Even better for me," she agrees. "C'mon. Let's get dried off and go to bed. We have an early morning tomorrow."

"Not until we at least get one more orgasm."

She quirks a brow at me. "For me or you?"

I smile back at her. "I'm not picky. Getting you off turns me on, so I'm happy either way."

"How about we both get each other off at the same time?"

"Then I'd say get your pretty ass into bed."

Chapter Twenty-Four

LYDIA

"Is it weird to be back in Boston?" Delaney asks.

Our bus snakes through the afternoon traffic as we depart from the hotel. She's sitting across the aisle from me. With a tablet in hand, it looks like we're reviewing film for the game this afternoon.

A completely innocent thing for a coach and player to be doing. With a game coming up, it's easy for us to be going over the upcoming match.

I watch the city out the window, looking at all the familiar sights. Red brick buildings. Little pubs on the corner. People bundled up on this winter day.

"You know, it's weird. It's familiar and different at the same time. Like the city has moved on without me."

"Does it still feel like home?"

I shake my head. "It doesn't. Even though I've only been in Toronto a few months, it feels more like home than Boston ever did."

"I wonder why."

Turning to look at her, there's a soft smile there.

She knows why.

It's because of her. While I wish I could have heard from my dad, it's not the end of the world today.

Because the little family that I have created with Parker, Skylar, Biscuit, and her makes Toronto feel like home. Getting traded is stressful for any player. But it hasn't been as hard as I thought. To top it off, my play has only gotten better since getting there which is the cherry on top.

"We're almost there," a voice shouts from the front of the bus.

"That's my cue." Delaney winks at me, dropping her tablet into her bag and slinging it over her shoulder.

Delaney walks to the front of the bus as we pull into the parking lot of the familiar rink. A place that used to be my home away from home.

Nerves bubble up inside of me.

That's a new feeling.

It's the first time I've been back here since I got traded. Sure, Boston has come to town to play in Toronto, but I didn't have these same feelings then.

I adjust the jersey I'm wearing over my patterned tights with a pair of black platform boots.

I slide into my leather jacket—not wanting something warmer for my walk-in since we'll only be outside for a minute or two.

Filing off the bus, Skylar and Parker flank my sides. The team's videographer is filming us as a few of the press that I recognize from my days here are snapping photos and talking to some of our players.

"Welcome back to Boston, Lydia," one of them calls my way.

"Good to be back."

"Lydia, do you think you're showing favoritism by wearing a Black Diamonds jersey? Shouldn't you be supporting the Toronto Sixers? They're playing tonight."

I plaster a fake smile on my face. Years of media training has prepped me for moments like this. "If it means I'm showing favoritism by supporting my brother's team, then so be it. I'm excited for them tonight because they can lock up their spot in the playoffs."

"Think you'll be doing that?"

"I hope so."

"Good luck out there."

I nod at the reporter, following the rest of the ladies down the tunnel toward the visitors' locker room.

Favoritism, I scoff.

As if. I'm supporting my brother. What a ridiculous question to ask. The Black Diamonds are killing it this season, so I'm going to support Troy and his team any way I can.

"Lydia. How are you?" An older man with a beaming smile approaches me, breaking me out of my straying thoughts.

"Hey, Coach."

He pulls me in for a hug. "I'm glad to see you haven't ignored everything I taught you when you went to Toronto."

"I might have remembered a thing or two. Something you'll be regretting later tonight."

"I see not much has changed."

"Just my team," I tell him.

He laughs. "We miss you, but we have a great team this year. Hopefully we'll beat the number one team in the league tonight."

"We're not going to make it easy for you," I say.

"I have no doubt." He gives me one last hug. "Take care of yourself, alright?"

"You too. It was nice seeing you."

He waves goodbye before heading down the hall to where the home locker rooms are.

Before I know it, pregame warm-ups are over and the game is starting. The lines are different, but I know a handful of these women. Know how they play. Their tells.

When one of their defenders tries to deke me out, it's easy to get around her, and I get an easy shot on goal to get the Rosebuds off to a 1-0 lead.

It's encouraging to hear the boos from the home crowd.

Not something I'm used to from here, but I'm glad because it means we're doing something right.

Boston doesn't take it lying down. They get an easy goal on Parker to tie it up in the first, but when we come back in the second, Skylar puts it in the goal.

It stays that way until the third period.

Both teams are fighting hard. When our line is up again, I'm leaping over the boards and flying across the ice. Taking the puck, I pass it to Skylar before she shoots it back to me. Before I can take off again, I'm being checked into the boards.

Fuck. *Fuck.*

The whistle blows, sending one of Boston's players—someone I don't know—to the sin bin.

That hit hurt. Breathing through the spike of pain, I skate back over to the bench.

"Feeling alright?" Delaney asks as I retake my seat.

"Good, Coach. Nothing I can't skate off."

I swipe my water bottle and take a gulp. Boston is able to kill the power play before they tie it up when their winger retakes the ice.

"Still a few minutes left to go. Lydia, Skylar. Head back out," Delaney calls out.

The two of us change up the lines. Our center is able

to steal the puck from them and we head to our zone. I push off my skates and stay skate for skate with them.

When the puck comes my way, I'm ready. Pulling my stick back, I fire it at the goal. It hits the crossbar and goes in.

"Yes!" I throw my arms up in celebration.

"Way to go, Bishop!" Skylar wraps me up in a hug as the rest of the girls pile on top.

"Hell, yeah! Let's bring it home," I tell them.

I skate back to center ice for the puck drop, and from here on out, we're on the defensive. Boston pulls their goalie with a minute left, but it doesn't help.

We're able to pull off the win.

"That was an incredible team win," Delaney tells us when we're all back in the locker room. "I'm proud of how you fought until the end and worked together as a team. Our defense was on fire tonight, and Lydia, that was a great goal to seal the win. I want you all to enjoy the win tonight, but be ready for a light workout tomorrow before we head to New York."

"You want to get a drink at the hotel bar?" Skylar asks.

"I'll do one." I wince as I pull my jersey and pads over my head. "Then I'm going to ice my side."

"It is a bit bruised," Parker says. "We need you in tip-top shape for tomorrow."

"I plan on it. So one drink."

"An actual drink?" Skylar asks. "Or something non-alcoholic?"

"I think one drink would be alright."

I change into my sweats in my bag and head out to the team bus. My phone buzzes in my pocket.

DELANEY

Want to come to my room tonight?

LYDIA

I thought you'd never ask

Try and sneak away when you can

I'm going to have a drink with the girls and then I'll be up

Can't wait

I CLOSE out of my texts and pull up my email app. Nothing from my dad. I sigh. So much for trying to see him while I'm here. Hell, I don't even know if he's in town.

My phone buzzes, and this alert has me smiling.

DEREK

Great shot to win the game, Lydia

MOM

How's your side? That looked like a hard hit

ANGIE

Cam was cheering hard for you <<pic of a sleeping baby>>

TROY

Hey, why not me?

ANGIE

She's in your jersey now <<pic of sleeping baby>>

TROY

That's better

LYDIA

She has to rep her favorite aunt!

MOM

How are you feeling?

Sore, but nothing a little pain reliever won't fix

MOM

And an ice pack. Keep that on there for a little while tonight. That'll help

Yes, Mom

MOM

I can hear that tone, young lady

TROY

Ouch. Mom calling you out via text

MOM

Only because I don't want her to overdo it

MOM

Good luck tonight, Troy

TROY

Thanks, Mom

DEREK

Fingers crossed for tonight!

TROY

I MIGHT NOT BE SEEING my dad anytime soon, but at least I have them. And Delaney. Who I can't wait to spend the night with.

Chapter Twenty-Five

It's going to be a good night.

After a fantastic afternoon win against Boston on their ice, we have the night off. I can't wait until Lydia sneaks up here later.

After taking a long, hot shower, I make myself a cocktail from the minibar and settle onto the mattress. Not the best one I've had on the road, but I don't care.

With a happy sigh, I sink into the down pillows. I'm usually not the biggest fan of overnights in hotel beds. I prefer my own, but tonight, I'll be glad to have some company.

For once, I don't plan what we have coming up. I don't immediately pull up film for our next opponent.

I enjoy the quiet.

I start to nod off before a knock sounds at the door.

Jumping off the bed, I look through the peephole and see Lydia looking both ways.

Opening the door, I pull her inside before anyone can spot her. "Hey."

"Hi."

Bringing her in close, I plant a kiss on her lips. But it doesn't get far before she winces.

"Are you okay?" I ask, pulling her Rosebuds sweatshirt up to investigate her side. A bruise mars her torso. Nothing huge, but it's still there.

"I'm okay." She pushes my hands away and lies down on the bed.

"Are you?"

"Well, I could use some ice. I already took pain reliever."

"Good." Grabbing the ice bucket, I take the bag of ice and wrap it in a towel from the bathroom.

"Let me."

I sit next to her, resting the ice on her side where the bruise is.

"I bet this isn't what you had in mind for tonight."

I steal a kiss. "I wanted to spend the night with you."

Lydia sighs and I lie down facing her.

"For once, I wish we were at home. I wouldn't mind having Biscuit here to curl up with us," she tells me. I know he stays with her neighbor while we're away.

"Would you rather have two-week road trips like the men's teams?"

She shakes her head, tucking her hands under the side of her face. "I'm good. I like our schedule."

"You want to put on a movie?"

"Sure."

Grabbing the remote, I flip to the movie channel and find a comedy to watch. An older movie that we don't have to pay attention to if we don't want to.

"This reminds me of when I was a kid," Lydia says.

"Lying in bed with a girlfriend watching a movie?"

She laughs. "No. Getting to stay up late and watch movies."

"Yeah?"

"Troy and I used to build these epic pillow forts in the living room whenever we got to stay up and watch a movie. We each got to pick a candy bar for a snack. They were some of my favorite days."

"Do you miss them?" I ask, tucking a lock of blonde hair behind her ear.

"Sometimes. The easier days when you didn't have to worry about your stats. Or how many goals you're getting so you can keep your starting position on the team."

"Are you worried about losing it?" I ask.

"No." She smiles. "But I miss the days of just being able to play for the fun of it. I mean, don't get me wrong, it's still fun. But there's more to it now."

"I know what you mean. Hell, I miss the days of being able to play."

"How did you deal with all of that changing in the blink of an eye?"

I flip onto my back, taking Lydia's hand in mine. I trace the lines of her palm. This is easier than looking at her.

"I didn't handle it all that well at the beginning. I thought all the doctors were wrong and that I knew better. I worked so hard on rehab and getting my leg better, but the strength just wasn't there."

"I wish I could have been there to help you," Lydia says.

"I don't think I could have handled that. I had tunnel vision. The only thing I did was rehab. Nothing else mattered."

"Did you stay with your mom while rehabbing?"

"Yeah. She was the only reason I stayed sane during that time."

Lydia gives me a small smile. "Did she ever try setting you up while you were healing? Maybe that could have helped you get better faster."

I can't hide my wince. "She…still doesn't know."

"You haven't told her?"

"I'm too scared," I confess. "She's all I have in the world. What if she disowns me? I don't want to lose her."

"I'm not going to lie; being disowned hurts."

"Who disowned you?"

She waggles her head. "Well, not really disowned. But I can't get my own father to see me."

"Who wouldn't want you in their life? You make everything brighter."

She smiles at me, pulling me close and cupping my cheek. "You're the exact same. You are kind and beautiful, D. And no matter what happens, you have more people in your life than you know. I love you, and I'm not planning on going anywhere."

"Do you realize what you just said?" My breath catches in my chest.

"That I love you? Yeah. And you don't have to say it back, but I want you to know. I love you, Del—"

I cut her off with a kiss, flipping her onto her back so the ice pack slides off her side onto the bed. It's a sweet and easy kiss, but one that is full of love and promise. Of what's to come in the future.

"I love you too. And I want to tell my mom about you, but—"

Lydia quiets me with a finger over my mouth. "You don't have to. Tell her when you're ready. I promise, I'm not going anywhere."

"I guess we're two peas in a pod. Your dad won't talk to you and I'm too scared to talk to my mom."

"We'll deal with it together."

Together. The best damn word I've heard in a long time. Having someone to do the hard things with.

Together.

Chapter Twenty-Six

I hate this. I've never been more miserable in my life. Curled up on the couch, watching the Rosebuds play, is not where I thought I'd be.

Catching the stomach bug is not what I wanted. For the past two days, I've been horizontal on the couch in my apartment.

We're currently down against Vancouver, but only by one. I hate that I can't be out on the ice helping my team.

Considering I can hardly stand, I wouldn't have been able to support them. Biscuit is stretched out on the floor in front of me. Half-drunk Gatorade sits on the coffee table as my phone buzzes.

"Hey, Mom."

"I'd ask how you're feeling, but you don't sound great," she says.

"I don't think I've ever felt more miserable in my life."

My stomach rumbles, but thankfully, nothing comes up this time.

"Do you need me to come out there and take care of you?" Mom asks.

"No, I'll be okay. It should go away by tomorrow."

I hope.

We're in a good position to make the playoffs, and the very last thing I want is to be sitting on the sidelines when that happens.

"I know it's hard, but stay hydrated and try to eat some crackers if you can keep them down."

I smile through the phone, even though she can't see me. Always the nurse taking care of her children.

"I will. Yes!"

"Are you watching the game?" Mom's laughter carries over the line.

Skylar just evened the score with an incredible goal from the top of the crease, set up by our center.

"Of course I am. I hate that I can't be there."

"Make sure you take care of yourself so you can get back on the ice sooner rather than later."

"I promise, I am."

"Okay, well, I just wanted to check on you. Call me when you're feeling better, okay, sweetie?"

"I will, Mom. Thanks. Love you."

"Love you."

I end the call, watching as Skylar puts another point on the board. The rest of the game picks up from there. I wish I could be out there with my team, but it looks like they're doing just fine without me, beating Vancouver 4-2.

It's one of the things that is harder with fewer than a dozen teams in the league. You get to know their playing skills better than you would with more teams so it's hard to get a competitive edge. I watch the postgame shows with Skylar and Delaney, talking about how they worked together as a team to pull off the win.

No professional athlete likes sitting out of the game,

but I'm happy for my team. They cut to the GM and owner as they congratulate Delaney on the win.

I swallow down the nerves that swell up in my belly that have nothing to do with the sickness.

What we're doing is against the rules. This whole thing between the two of us could explode in our faces.

We shouldn't be doing this, but when I see a text flash across my phone from her, it's hard to put a voice to those reasons and end this.

Because all I want is Delaney.

DELANEY

Feel like some company tonight?

I SMILE as I punch out a response.

LYDIA

Yes

Want to come over and tell me all about your big win?

If you saw it, we don't need to talk about it

I want to hear how you kicked ass

I'll see your pretty ass in an hour or so

Can't wait

XOXO

I SET the phone down and let Biscuit out on the outdoor patio. One of the perks of the apartment is the large outdoor space with artificial turf. It's the perfect space for him when I can't take him outside for a longer walk. It's like he knows I'm sick and doesn't want to stray too far from me, curling up at my feet when we come back inside.

DELANEY

I'm here

I BUZZ her up and wait by the door with Biscuit. When she steps off the elevator and she spots me, her face falls.

"Wow, you really don't look good."

"Gee, thanks." I sweep my arm out for her to come in. "I talked to my mom during the game and she said I sounded terrible."

"That too. We only say it out of love." Biscuit is spinning in circles around her feet, yapping at her. "Hi, Biscuit. I missed you too. Are you taking good care of your mom?"

"He was a good Rosebuds fan tonight. Cheering the team on as you locked up a playoff spot."

Delaney smiles. "Are you upset we did it without you?"

"Why would I be upset? The only reason I'm upset is we can't celebrate tonight."

"I need you at full strength so we can make it all the way."

"I know—"

My stomach rumbling cuts me off. This time it's not a false alarm as I run to the bathroom.

I make it just in time. It feels like all I've been doing today is worshipping the porcelain god.

"What do you need?" A warm hand settles on my lower back. "Can I get you anything?"

"Can you make it stop?" I rest my cheek on my forearm and peek one eye up at her. "I can't tell you the last time I've felt so miserable."

"I'm sorry you're feeling so crappy." She brushes a stray lock of hair off my sticky forehead.

My eyes close at her soft touch.

"Maybe you should head home. I don't want you getting sick."

Delaney rubs circles on my back. "C'mon. Let's get you into bed. I'll make sure you get to sleep and then I'll head home."

"I hope no one else on the team gets sick, but if it's only you, it might seem fishy."

"I won't stay long." Delaney grabs a washcloth and wets it down. "Let's go."

Grabbing her extended hand, I let her pull me up and lead me into the bedroom. She peels back the comforter and I slide in.

"Thank you."

She presses the damp cloth on my head and my eyes flutter shut. Damn, does that ever feel good.

"I want you to drink a little bit of Gatorade before I leave."

"Yes, Mom." I laugh.

"Hey, I want to make sure you don't get dehydrated."

I smile, even though I can't see her face. "My mom has told me that several times today via text and when she called earlier."

"We care. We want you to get better."

"I love you," I whisper.

"I know. I love you too."

"I wish this was more of a fun night to celebrate."

"There will be plenty of other nights we can celebrate our big win."

"Hopefully this won't keep me down too much longer," I say.

Delaney starts dragging her fingers along my scalp, and the combination of that and the cool cloth on my head starts to pull me under.

"You sleep. I'll come back and see you when you're feeling better." I feel Delaney's lips against my head as Biscuit curls up next to me.

"Thank you for taking care of me."

"Always. I will always take care of you, Lyd."

And it's that thought that carries me to sleep.

Delaney taking care of me.

God, did I ever get lucky.

Chapter Twenty-Seven

LYDIA

DELANEY

Are you still planning on coming over tonight?

LYDIA

I was planning on it

Good

You know, I could always come over earlier

Our coach oh so generously gave us the day off from practice after a winning streak this weekend

Your coach is too easy on you

I don't know about that

One practice off? I wouldn't go that far

Har har

I'll see you tonight

. . .

The coffee shop is bustling. People working. Friends meeting. Moms with kids having breakfast. Warmth and the smell of coffee permeates the air. It's the perfect way to spend the morning off now that I'm feeling better.

Burrowing farther into the oversized chair, I sip on my tea and watch everyone coming and going in the shop.

Until I see someone I never thought I'd see in my little neighborhood.

He's tapping away on his phone. Considering I haven't seen him in about a year, he looks about the same. Maybe a bit more gray around the temples, but I'd recognize him in a heartbeat.

His suit is immaculate—a navy pinstripe suit with shiny Oxford shoes.

"Dad?"

The man in a suit stops, looking around to see who called out. When his blue eyes spot me, he looks stunned. "Lydia? What are you doing here?"

"What am I doing here? I live here."

"You live here now? Why?" He glances down at his phone again, then looks at the counter to see if they've called his name for his order.

"Hockey. I told you I got traded here to the new women's team."

His lips flatten into a grim line. "I thought you put all that hockey nonsense behind you."

"Is that what you think of it?" I scoff. "I'm one of the top five players in the league right now."

"Not the top?" He quirks a brow at me.

I mean, I am, but for some reason, I don't feel the need to tell that to this man. The man that couldn't even bother texting me to tell me he's in town.

How is this the man that I've been fighting to get a scrap of attention from for all these years?

"I—"

"I have to go," he interrupts, hearing his name called. "Nice seeing you, Lydia."

"Wait." I call out after him. He stops, spinning on his heel with a look of annoyance on his face. "How long are you in town? Can we get dinner?"

"Sorry. I have meetings."

He leaves without another word.

My dad. The man who left when I was four. Who never seemed that interested in my life. Who, no matter what I seemed to do to keep him in my life, was never around.

So why does it hurt so much when I had the best step-dad, mom, and stepbrother growing up? I never wanted for anything.

The only thing I share with this man is DNA. Is that enough of a reason to want to have someone in your life?

I shouldn't care, but I do.

My phone buzzes in my pocket, and I don't see who's calling before I decline it. Too many emotions are swimming inside me.

So much for enjoying my morning off.

Swallowing down the rest of my tea, I set my empty cup down in the bin by the door and head out into the cold Toronto morning. Snow sticks to the sidewalk as I try to get my bearings.

I hate that I'm letting him get to me. I have too much going on right now to worry about it. Toronto is kicking ass and that should be my *only* worry. Keeping us in the running to make it to the finals our first year.

My phone buzzes again. This time, pulling it out, I see it's my mom calling.

"Hey, Mom."

"What's wrong, sweetie?"

I sigh. There is no use hiding anything from my mom. It's like she has a sixth sense for when anything is wrong with one of her kids. I don't know how she does it.

"I saw Dad."

"You did?" She can't hide the shock from her voice. "Why didn't you tell me you were going to see him?"

"Because I didn't know." I turn the corner and head toward the rink. I'm so worked up now, there's no use in going home. I might as well get a workout in to try and get all these feelings of mine under control.

"He was in Toronto and he didn't reach out to you?" Bitterness laces her voice. My mom is the kindest person out there. The one person in the world she can't stand? Her ex-husband.

"He was surprised I was still even playing hockey. Called it nonsense."

"I could kill him." She's muttering under her breath, but I'm not catching most of it. "I'm sorry, sweetie. I wish he weren't like this. I wish he cared more."

"It's not your fault." The crosswalk blinks red and I stop. Given that the temps have dropped, there aren't many people out and about today. "I just wish I didn't keep having hope he'd be different."

A frustrated tear slips out. I wipe it away with anger.

"I wish he was a better father to you, Lydia. I do."

"It's not like I don't have Derek," I tell her. "I have you."

"He's still your father, dear." She sighs. "Is there anything I can do?"

I shake my head, even though she can't see me. "No. I'm going to get a workout in."

Mom laughs. "Of course you are."

"Hey." The light changes and I cross the road. "It helps clear my head."

"I know it does. I just wish you were able to go visit your brother with us next week. Baby snuggles are always good to make you feel better."

My heart clatters around in my chest. "I know. You'll just have to take all the pictures and videos and send them to me."

It's the one thing that sucks about being a professional hockey player. When my family is going to visit Troy and Angie, I'm here because of games and practice. And after seeing my dad today? I really could use some family time.

"We will, but I can always come there if you need me to," Mom says.

"That's okay, Mom. Go and visit Cam and I'll see you soon enough." The arena is in front of me. "Look, I'm here. I'll call you later, okay?"

"Okay. I love you, dear. You know where I am if you need anything."

I smile. "Thanks. I love you. Bye."

I end the call, feeling a bit better after talking with her.

The rink is empty. After the two wins back to back, Delaney gave us the day off from practice, so no one is here.

Heading to my locker, I shed my coat and put on my white skates. The ones I keep here for when I need to come and think things through.

The ice is a blank slate as I walk through the gate and take off. I push into the blades, needing to feel the burn in my legs.

How is that man my father? After trying to connect with him so often, he cares that little about me? And why do I care so much?

"Are you okay?"

I swish to a stop, covering the boards in ice. Delaney is skating toward me, a worried look on her face.

"It's my dad."

"Derek? Is he okay?"

"No, not him. My real dad."

"Your real dad?"

I nod, trying to take off again, but Delaney stops me with a hand to the elbow.

"He was here in Toronto."

"He was?"

"Yup." I pop the *p*. "And he didn't even bother to tell me that he was here."

"Lydia. I'm so sorry."

My fingers grasp her elbows, digging into the soft black material of the oversized turtleneck she's wearing with a pair of leggings.

"How can the man who helped create me care so little about me?" A frustrated tear slips out. "It's not like I don't have good memories with him from when I was little."

I remember the time he took me to the zoo and we got ice cream—a splurge at the time. Or snacks at the movies. But if it's only a few memories here and there, can I even call him my dad?

"He doesn't deserve your tears." Delaney wipes it away as another takes its place.

I bite down on my bottom lip. I don't want to cry, but I can't help it.

"Hey. It's going to be okay."

Delaney pulls me into her arms and I bury my face in her shoulder. It triggers the cascade of tears as I hold on to her.

"This man has basically been out of my life since I was a teenager." My voice is thick with emotion. "He never understood why I loved hockey. He called it nonsense. Why am I so torn up over this when the last time we had a real relationship was when I was in middle school?"

"Because"—Delaney pulls back, brushing the tears away—"he is supposed to love you and has shown you time and time again that he doesn't. That kind of rejection hurts. No one wants it."

"No," I blurt out. "I guess I have my answer. He doesn't care, so I guess I have to move on."

"You don't have to do it alone, Lydia. I'm here for you. Parker and Skylar are here for you. Your entire family is. You're not alone."

"God, I love you, Delaney. I kept fighting for this idea of a family that I was never going to have. I guess I just wanted him to be proud of me."

"The people who matter are."

"Thank you." I drop my forehead to hers. "Thank you, D."

"Like I said, I'm here for you. Whatever you need."

"You. Just you, Delaney."

Delaney pulls back, releasing the tether I have on her. "Why don't we go back to your place? Get takeout and get lost in one another?"

"Right. Probably not the best place to be doing this."

I wipe one last stray tear away. I hate that I'm wasting any tears on that man. He doesn't deserve them. He proved to me that he doesn't, but it's going to take some time to work through that.

"Or maybe if you want, you can go hit one of the boxing bags in the training room to work out your feelings?"

I smile at her. "I like your first idea better."

"Good. Me too."

"See you at home?"

Delaney skates away from me. "See you at home."

Chapter Twenty-Eight

DELANEY

"Okay. See here how this defender always drops back too far when they enter the zone? We can capitalize on that," I tell Nadia.

"Yes. We'll work on attacking drills today in practice."

"Good. Minneapolis is going to be a hard team to beat."

"We've got this, Delaney," Nadia says.

"Excuse me, Ms. Charles?"

I glance up to see the general manager's assistant standing in the doorway of my office.

"Yes? How can I help you?"

"Mr. Tremblay would like to see you in his office."

"Oh. Okay. Is everything alright?"

Nerves burst in my gut. Why does the GM want to see me?

"I was told to come and get you."

I pass the tablet to Nadia. "If I'm not back, go ahead and get practice started."

"Sounds good." She gives me a reassuring smile, but it doesn't do much to reassure me.

As I follow the assistant toward the executive offices, dread slides down my throat. I have been in the GM's office once. When I signed the paperwork to officially accept the position of head coach of the Rosebuds.

He'll randomly drop by practice, and I'll see him after the games, but never in such a formal manner.

Except…oh God. Is this about Lydia?

Fuck.

Fuck.

What else could they be calling me in for?

Stay calm, Delaney. You don't know what this is about. No sense in borrowing trouble.

Maybe there's a new player they traded for? Yes. That must be it.

I wish the woman would hurry up. I can't take it. Each step feels like I'm moving backward. I just want to get this meeting over with. Rip the Band-Aid off and all.

She waves me toward Mr. Tremblay's office as we walk into the executive suite.

"He's expecting you. Go on in."

"Thank you." I try to manage a smile, but it comes out as more of a grimace.

Great. I don't think this is going to go well. I knock on the door, and his voice beckons me in.

Not only is the GM in here, but the owner as well.

"Hi. Am I interrupting?"

"Delaney. We needed to speak with you. Please, take a seat so we can discuss a few things with you."

I take the seat across from him. Neither one of them looks pleased.

"What can I help you with?" I ask.

"Delaney, it's come to our attention that you've broken the no fraternization policy with one of your players."

"Okay." I clear my throat.

How in the world did they find out?

I keep my face calm. No sense in showing all of my emotions and giving myself away.

"What do you have to say for yourself?"

"We were called by one of the team reporters asking for a comment on your relationship."

"With whom?" I ask.

The two of them exchange a look.

"We will have photographic evidence within the next forty-eight hours," Mr. Allen says.

"So you don't have anything?" I ask, trying to clarify what I'm hearing.

"We will. Do you have anything to say for yourself?" Mr. Tremblay asks.

"I would like to see this evidence before I say anything."

I don't want to incriminate myself. What if it's a photo with another player that was taken out of context? Lydia and I are two consenting adults in a relationship even if it's violating the team's policy. We both knew we were breaking the rules, but we didn't care because we're in love. But if these photos show anything with Lydia? We're screwed.

Well, I'm screwed.

Mr. Tremblay taps on his phone. "We take all of these allegations very seriously. Until we have a chance to investigate more thoroughly, you will be placed on leave. You are expected to come into the office Friday morning at eight where we will have a further discussion on this."

"I can assure you, this is all a big misunderstanding," I tell them, hoping against hope that it is.

"We hope so. But until then, we ask that you leave the premises. Your assistant coaches will be informed shortly that they will be taking over the team until further notice."

"Right."

"That's all."

I take the dismissal for what it is and scurry out of the office. How did we get ourselves into this situation?

I'm a rule follower. I never break the rules. But when Lydia looked at me, I was putty in her hands. She was always the one that got away. When our lips touched, I couldn't think of anything else but her. Of wanting to be with her. Of wanting to spend all my time with her. And now it's possible there are photos of us out in the world.

This is not what I needed today.

Bile rises in my throat as I hurry back to my office to grab my bag and keys. At this point, practice will have already started.

Will Lydia be out there wondering where I am? After an emotionally charged night at the rink, we spent the night together before leaving separately for practice.

There's no way someone saw us together last night. Only the team has access to the rink after hours.

Fuck. I hate this. I really do.

Everything I've ever wanted was in reach.

Now? It's all going to blow up in my face.

Chapter Twenty-Nine

LYDIA

To say practice was a shit show is an understatement.

When Bailey said she was taking over for Delaney, my mind went to worst-case scenarios. Everything was fine when the two of us left my place.

I have no idea what happened between then and now.

And it showed.

Missed passes. Shots going wide. Sluggish.

I was not my usual self. Thankfully, Bailey chalked it up to me recovering from illness.

"You okay?" Parker asks as I finish towel drying my hair. "You seemed off today."

"Just tired. I think I might have pushed myself too hard coming back."

"Too tired to grab dinner tonight?"

"I'm going to have to take a raincheck." I grab my coat and bag. "But thanks."

"You sure you're okay?" Parker asks again.

"Nothing a good night's sleep won't cure." I smile at her.

"And some Biscuit snuggles."

"That too."

"I'll see you tomorrow."

I wave goodbye and head out of the arena. I wait until I'm clear to pull my phone out. A text from Delaney is waiting.

DELANEY

Come to my place

THAT DOESN'T SOUND GOOD. Fuck. It doesn't do anything to calm my jangled nerves.

LYDIA

Heading to you now

EACH MOMENT to her place seems endless. Traffic is terrible as usual. I wish I could beam myself there, but I can't.

By the time her house comes into view, I'm throwing my car in park and dashing up to the front door. Testing the lock, it's open and I push in.

"Delaney?" I don't have to look far for her. She's pacing in the kitchen when I get inside. "What's wrong?"

"They know about us." I notice the cocktail in her hand.

"What? How?"

She sips the drink. "I got called to the GM's office

today. He said there were allegations of me having inappropriate relations with one of my players."

"Oh God. What did they say?"

"They said there are photos."

"Did you see them?" I ask.

"No. They were asked for a comment and then told the pictures were forthcoming. I have another meeting with the team on Friday morning. This is bad, Lydia. Really bad."

What she's saying does nothing to calm my nerves. It only makes the nauseous feeling swell…because what if I lose this job?

"Okay. We don't know what it is yet. Let's not get ahead of ourselves."

"What else could it be?" she asks.

"Let's say they have photos of us, which I'm not saying they do. Do you think we could say they were old photos?"

Delaney scoffs. "I don't know if it would look any better if I hid a past relationship with one of my players."

"It's not like you were my coach then."

"They could fire me. They *will* fire me. And what would I tell my mother if I lose my job?"

"Breathe, Delaney." I rush over to her, stopping her pacing. "Let's look at this rationally."

She drops her forehead to mine. "How?"

"We don't know what they have. Should they have called you into the office without the evidence and let you stew over this for the next two days? No. But it could all be nothing."

"And if it's not?"

"Look, Delaney, if you have the chance to save your job, I want you to take it."

"I don't want to hide you."

I shake my head. "No. I don't want to hide our relationship either. But if you get fired, you won't be able to stay in Toronto. And with our schedules, it'd be nearly impossible to see each other."

"God." Delaney pulls out of my arms and starts pacing again. "And what will the team say if they find out we're together?"

"It'll be okay."

"Will it?" She shoves a hand through her hair. "This is all a mess."

"What are you saying?" I ask, dread now swimming in my stomach.

"I don't know, Lyd. I really don't."

I stop her with a hand on her stomach. "I'll clear things up then. I want you. Only you."

That earns me a soft smile. "I want you too."

"So then we're going to have to figure out a way to deal with this."

"When I'm shipped off to a small division three school in New Mexico and you're here in Toronto living out your dream."

I sigh, wishing I could stop Delaney from spiraling, but I don't think I can. With the threat of losing her job hanging over her, there's not much I can say.

Because it feels like an impossible situation.

It's either Delaney's job or us. Either way, we're going to lose.

"Are we going to solve this problem right now?" I ask.

Delaney stops and stares at me like I've lost my mind. "No. But I don't think we'll solve it by Friday either."

"Then why don't we get lost in each other? Remember why we started this thing? We're two people who love each other, and that's the most important thing."

Taking my hand, Delaney leads me upstairs. The two of us shed our clothes before falling into bed, wrapped in each other's arms.

Our kisses are fraught and hurried. Hands are searching as I slide two fingers inside of her. Delaney's thumb strums my clit. We know exactly how to get each other off.

This entire day has gone to shit, but at least we can get out of our heads for a little while as we work each other over until we spill over the edge.

We're naked and breathing hard as we're wrapped in each other's arms.

"Whatever happens, will happen," I say, pressing a kiss to Delaney's bare shoulder. "But we'll face it together."

"Promise?"

"Always. You're not alone in this, Delaney. I'm here for you."

"Good. Because I love you."

"I love you too."

Chapter Thirty

DELANEY

"Does this say I'm fighting for my job? Or just straight-up fire me?" I step out of the closet, modeling not my first outfit for Lydia this morning.

"It's going to be okay," Lydia tells me. "They won't fire you."

"I wish I had that confidence." I fiddle with one of the buttons on my pink blouse. "It feels like they're going to fire me."

Wrapping her arms around me, Lydia pulls me in for a hug. "Remember what I said. We don't know what they have, and this could all be a big misunderstanding."

I scoff. "I doubt that." I step back, taking Lydia in. Her brows are pinched, mouth drawn tight. "And that face doesn't exactly scream confidence."

"Sorry. I'm nervous for you."

"Me too."

I untuck the blouse I'm wearing and go back in and find a yellow one. Yellow seems safe.

"God, this sucks," Lydia says from the bedroom. "It's not like you gave me any preferential treatment."

"But that's the problem. What if someone thinks you got more ice time than they did?"

"As if. You'd be more likely to reduce my playing time if I make you mad."

"I'm being serious."

"I am too." A smirk plays on the corner of her mouth. A moment of brevity in what is going to be a hard day. "If I pulled some dumb move, you wouldn't hesitate to put me in my place."

This time, I sweep her into my arms and keep her there. "Well, someone has to keep this ego in check."

"Hey. I can back it up. I'm still leading the league in most goals this season."

I sigh, my heart tightening in my chest. I don't know what is going to happen today, but I don't know if I can keep this.

It seems I only just got Lydia back and I'm going to lose her again.

Fuck.

"I wish this were easier."

"I know." Lydia cups my cheek. "I'm sorry I put you in this position."

"No. I wanted this. Trust me. I'm an adult and make my own decisions." I shake my head. "And now we have to face the consequences of our decision."

Lydia kisses me and it helps to calm some of my nerves. But only some. "I'm serious. I love you, Delaney, but if you see an opening to keep your job, I want you to take it. The Rosebuds need you."

"I need *you*."

"And you'll always have me," she says, eyes glancing at the clock. "But you need to go so you're not late."

"Right." I steal a kiss before going over to the bed to

pet Biscuit. "I'm going to be awhile, I'm guessing, so meet me back here this afternoon?"

She nods. "I'm going to go home and get more things for Biscuit, go for a quick run, and I'll be back over."

"Good. I love you."

"I love you too."

X

NOT FOR THE FIRST TIME, I'm sitting in the corporate offices for the Toronto Rosebuds. The first time, I was being interviewed for the coaching job.

Now? Now, I'll be lucky to keep that job.

I knew what starting a relationship with Lydia would entail. A head coach and a player? It's off-limits. Any player could cry misconduct because I favor her over them.

Unless I deny everything, I don't see a way I'm going to walk out of here with my position intact.

Lydia is the star of the league. There's no way they're dropping her. Besides, I'm pretty sure there is something in my contract about morality.

Probably should have read it a bit closer.

Not that it would have mattered.

I've loved Lydia since the day I met her. There was never any hope to not have her in my life.

"Ms. Charles."

Lydia's words bang around in my head as I follow the secretary to the same conference room I interviewed in. The park beyond is covered in snow, even in late February.

"Thank you for coming in, Delaney," Mr. Tremblay starts.

I give him a grim smile. It's not like I had much of a choice, but I don't tell him that.

"As you can see from these photos, it looks like you're in a romantic relationship with Miss Bishop."

Photos from our trip to Miami are placed in front of me on the table. Ones of us outside the hotel and at dinner.

The very same trip that they sanctioned.

"Delaney. This is a serious offense. Do you care to state your relationship with Ms. Bishop?" Mr. Allen asks.

Lydia said to deny. If I can save my job, do it. These photos? They were taken before we had a relationship. I can say that with the utmost honesty.

But…then we couldn't continue what we have now.

For the first time, I feel comfortable in my own skin. That I don't have to deny who I love to the world.

"We're dating."

"You're not denying you're in a relationship with your player?"

I shake my head. "Mr. Tremblay and Mr. Allen, I respect both of you too much to lie. These photos were taken when Miss Bishop was my player. It was a scouting trip you sent me on with her. But the two of us have a history."

"You do?" Mr. Tremblay asks, looking more confused.

"Yes. We played together on the national team, as I'm sure you knew. But we had a relationship then. It ended when I got injured, but I never got over Lydia. These photos were innocent, but I'm not going to deny what she means to me now."

"And what is that?"

Could I really look the woman I love in the face and not tell her how desperately I'm in love with her? What's worse…the thought of losing my job, or losing Lydia again?

I lost Lydia once. I don't think I can go through that again.

"We're in love. And while I realize telling you this will jeopardize my position with the team, I hope that hers will not be in jeopardy."

Did I make an error in judgment falling for my player? Yes. But we're two consenting adults, and I do not want to deny myself the woman I love.

"I understand," Mr. Tremblay says. "Then Miss Charles—"

"Can I say something?" I hold out my hand to stop him.

He looks irritated at my request, but nods his head.

"This isn't a cavalier decision. I fell in love with Lydia when the two of us were playing together years ago, and I never stopped loving her. I love this team too much to lie to you. I never made a decision that put her above the team. And while you have no way of knowing or accepting that, I always put the team first. I will always consider it an honor to have coached the Rosebuds, but for the first time, I have the chance to follow my heart, and that's what I have to do."

His lips are spread into a thin, grim line. "You will be missed, Miss Charles. We appreciate you not making this decision harder than it needs to be."

"I'm sorry it had to come to this."

I shake their hands and leave the office.

Instead of leaving to a sense of joy like the day I was first here, this time, I'm leaving with a sense of dread. I have no job. Lydia's future is here with the Rosebuds. Hell, she's on a three-year contract. All I've ever wanted to do is coach in the PWHL. Even with the league expanding, there aren't any open positions. They're at a premium.

And who is going to want a coach that fell in love with one of their players?

My future is up in the air. I have Lydia, but how in the world am I going to tell my mother that I lost my job? All I told her was that it's been a tough week, but right now? I can't bring myself to talk to her.

And right now, I can't go home. I need air. I need to walk off the energy thrumming through me.

With no job and no prospects, things feel heavy.

At least I have Lydia…

Chapter Thirty-One

LYDIA

My feet pound against the pavement. The sound of my breathing echoes in my ears as I fill my lungs. Cold stings my cheeks from the wind whipping across the water. It's the only thing keeping me going right now. Because focusing on anything else is going to pull me under.

Damn it.

Grinding to a halt, I rest my hands on my hips as I take in the bay.

It's been a long week. And this morning feels like the longest part of it. I keep looking at my watch, wondering if her meeting has ended.

I hate this. I hate that we're in this situation and that there's no way out except to deny it or for her to be fired.

Do I want her to deny our relationship? No, of course not. But if it means she keeps her job and stays in Toronto? Well, I guess we'll cross that bridge when we get there.

I could be worrying about nothing, but why would they call her into their office if they *didn't* have something?

Why can't I have everything I love? Hockey and Delaney?

As if I didn't have enough to worry about, I'm still working through processing my feelings about cutting my dad out of my life.

Not that he would know. That would require him to acknowledge me in any way. It shouldn't hurt, but it does.

Between that, worrying about Delaney, *and* focusing on practice, I'm ready for the week to be over.

Turning back, I run all out toward my apartment building. It's cold and I'm ready to get inside and warm up.

But when I get to my building, I'm shocked at who's at my doorway.

"Derek?"

My stepdad is there waiting for me, knocking on the door.

"Lydia."

"What are you doing here?"

"Thought you could use your dad."

I rush to him, needing the comfort more than I thought. "I'm so glad you're here."

"Your mom said it's been a hard week."

"And I didn't tell her the half of it."

"Why don't I make you breakfast and you can tell me all about it?" he asks.

I nod and let us inside.

Before he can even pull the eggs and bacon out of the fridge, Biscuit is jumping all around him wanting attention. Me? Everything starts spilling out. From dating Delaney to my dad to Delaney's future with the team.

One thing that Derek is good at doing is listening. Whenever I was having a hard time, he was the person I would talk to.

"That's quite a lot to process." He passes over a plate

of sunny-side up eggs with a side of bacon and a mug of coffee.

"Sorry, that was a lot. Why'd you come out here?"

He settles onto the barstool next to me with a mug of coffee.

"I thought that much was obvious." He smiles, waving a hand in the air. "After all that, I figured you'd be trying to process everything with your dad."

My lip quivers. "I think that part stings the most."

"I never liked him."

"That's because he ran out on Mom and me." I roll my eyes and bite into the perfectly crisped piece of bacon.

"Yes, but he never showed me that he wanted to have a place in your life. You deserve people who fight for you, sweetheart. You don't want people who don't care. Who act like you're not important."

I swallow down the emotions threatening to take over.

Is that what I did to Delaney?

I was trying to make things easier for her. For us. But was I really saying she's not important? God, I'm such an idiot.

"I think I did that to Delaney," I confess, dropping the bacon strip.

"Trying to save a future isn't the same thing as acting like someone isn't important."

I squeeze Derek again, needing another hug. "I'm really glad you came."

"I love you, dear, and will always come whenever you need your dad."

A thought occurs to me. Something that I once thought about back in college, but never really revisited.

"About that."

"About what?" He sips his coffee, his brown eyes studying me with worry.

"I don't want any connection to the man that doesn't care about me. I mean, he didn't even know I was here and called my job nonsense."

Derek smiles. "I had to hold your mother back from tracking him down and burying him alive."

"Sounds about right." I laugh. "But he's not my dad. You are."

"And I always will be." He squeezes my hand. Tears line his eyes.

"You were always the one to bandage my bruised knees and take me to hockey practice. You cared when I came home from school upset about something. You were one of the first people I told about getting the position with the national team. You've been there for every important moment in my life."

"Where are you going with this?" Now he's really confused.

"I want to change my name."

"You do?"

I nod. "I don't want to be a Bishop anymore. That man deserves nothing from me. You do. My *real* dad."

Derek pulls me in for a tight hug. "I would be honored if you took the Hollins name."

"Good. Because I want to officially be a member of the family."

He laughs, pulling back and wiping a few tears away. "Like you weren't the one that welcomed me into the family first."

"I was six when you met Mom."

"And if you didn't like me, we wouldn't be here today."

I smile at him. "I think I liked you because I really wanted a sibling."

"The truth finally comes out." He bursts out laughing.

"Whatever name you have, you are always my daughter. That will never change."

"Thank you, Dad."

Before I can give him another hug, the buzzer from the front door sounds. "Sorry, let me get that."

As I'm walking over to the door, Delaney's voice echoes over the intercom. "Let me up?"

"Yeah." I press the button. "Do you think that's a bad sign?"

Derek shrugs a shoulder. "Don't jump to conclusions just yet."

"Easy for you to say."

He sips his coffee as the elevator door dings. Delaney comes rushing out and sweeps me into a hug before I can get a word in.

"What happened?"

"I—"

"Sorry to interrupt, but I'm going to head out."

Derek grabs his bag from the entryway before stopping.

"But you just got here."

He kisses my head. "And I have to check into the hotel. I'll get settled in and then why don't we all go out to dinner? Or I can pick something up and bring it over here."

"Thanks, Dad."

"I love you, sweetheart."

"I love you too."

He's gone, shutting the door behind him. Delaney looks at me with confusion lining her face.

"What happened here?"

"C'mon. We have a lot to talk about."

Chapter Thirty-Two

DELANEY

"**W**hat happened?" The second the door closes behind Derek, she's on me. "Do you still have a job? Are we still…an us?"

I shake my head. "I got fired."

"What'd they have on you?"

I swallow back the panic that's been steadily rising in my throat since I left the arena.

"It was pictures from dinner in Miami."

"Wait." Lydia looks stunned. "We weren't even together then."

I roll my eyes. "By a few hours or so."

"You could have easily denied it." She grabs my hands. "That would have been a true statement and you wouldn't have been lying."

"But we've been lying since then," I clarify, not that she doesn't know that. "I didn't want to. You're too important."

Lydia pulls me in tight for a hug. "I'm sorry if telling you to deny us made you feel less important than you are to me. Because you're not."

"I know."

"I was just trying to find a way to keep you any way I could."

I give her a half-hearted smile. "Well, at least for now, you'll have me all the time."

"Good."

"Can we walk to my place? Sorry, I have a lot of nervous energy I need to walk off," I ask.

"Sure."

Grabbing our coats and Biscuit's leash, the three of us head off on the walk that would normally be too long for us to make. But right now, it's exactly what I need.

"I wonder what they're going to tell the team," Lydia says.

I blow out a breath, the cold wind smacking us in the face as we leave her building. "I guess that's not something I have to worry about. Or studying film."

"Hey." She squeezes my hand. "You'll still be studying film. I have no doubt that you'll keep coaching me. And I'm sorry."

"For what?"

"That you have to take the brunt in all of this and that I can stay with the team."

"Well, you better win a championship."

We stop at a crosswalk. "Don't worry, I will."

The two of us walk in silence. Both of us seem wrapped up in our thoughts until I remember.

"What was Derek doing here?"

"He came to check on me," she says.

"After your douche of a dad was here?"

She nods. "Yeah. Which made me realize that I was fighting for something that was never there. He didn't care about me, but I kept wanting him to want me because what parent wouldn't want their child?"

"I'm sorry he was so terrible to you. You, Lydia Bishop, are the most incredible woman in the world and worth knowing."

"Well, you're almost right."

"Almost?" I question. "You're telling me you're not the most incredible woman in the world?"

She shakes her head. "I think you are, but that's not the point I'm contesting."

"What is?"

"Lydia Bishop. I'm changing my name."

"You are? Do you have something against the name of Lydia?"

"Bishop. I'm changing my name to Hollins."

"What made you decide this?"

We stop as Biscuit does his business. I tuck a loose strand of hair behind her ear. Her face is makeup free. Soft. She's so damn beautiful that I have to thank my lucky stars that I got a second chance with her.

"I realize I have no ties to Bishop. He's not my dad. Derek is. I want to be an official Hollins."

I wrap her in my arms. "Well, maybe in a few years you could change your name again."

"You're assuming I'll take your name if we get married?"

"Yes," I say, matter-of-factly.

"And what if I want you to take mine? Or we each just keep our own names?"

"I'll love you whatever your name is."

"Even if I want to change it to Queen of the Milky Way?"

"Ugh. Really?" I bury my head in her shoulder.

"I see your love for me has limits then."

I kiss her forehead. The tip of her nose. The corner of her mouth. "No. No limits. I'll love you always. Even if

I have to call you the most ridiculous names on the planet."

"Milky Way."

"Even then."

"I love you, Delaney. I'll spend every day making sure you know how much I love you because you do the same for me and I don't even think you realize it."

A throat clears and I spin on my heel, not even realizing that we're already at my front stoop.

Oh shit.

"Mom. What are you doing here?"

Lydia bumps into my back as I stop short of the stairs leading up to my front door.

"Mom? This is your mom?" Lydia whispers behind me.

"What do you mean what am I doing here?" Sunglasses cover her eyes so I can't see what she's looking at. "When you called, you seemed down in the dumps so I decided to come see you. I didn't want you to be alone and thought that you could use some cheering up. But it doesn't seem like you're alone…"

I swallow back the bile rising in my throat. This is so *not* how I saw my day going. Losing my job and my mom seeing me with Lydia?

I'm at a loss of what to do.

"Umm, let's go inside."

Walking past her, I give her a quick hug before opening the front door. She follows me in, with Lydia following her.

"I know it's early, but I think we might need something to drink," Mom says, dropping her bags in the entryway and heading straight for the kitchen.

Oh God. This really doesn't bode well for me.

"Are you okay?" Lydia asks.

"I…"

Am I okay? I have no idea. Not until I know what to expect from this conversation with my mother.

"Hey." Lydia grabs my hand and squeezes it. "No matter what happens, we're in this together, okay?"

I nod. "I love you."

She smiles back at me. "I love you too."

"Whatever you tell her, I'll support you," Lydia says.

"I just didn't expect her to land on my doorstep today." A nervous puff of air escapes my lips.

"She's a good mother. I have a feeling she'll surprise you." Lydia winks at me.

"Can I get you anything?" Mom calls from the kitchen.

"Just water, please."

The two of us walk into the kitchen and each take a seat on the barstools.

"Delaney, your usual?"

"Yes, please."

I don't care that it's not even one in the afternoon yet. I lost my job and I hope to God my mom doesn't walk out of here hating me because of who I love.

I need a drink.

"Well, I know who you are," Mom tells Lydia as she starts pulling out all the ingredients.

"You do?" Lydia looks confused. "How do you know me?"

She scoffs. "As if I don't watch every Rosebuds game."

Lydia takes the water that Mom slides across the counter. "I'm glad you do."

"Am I still going to be watching them?" She quirks a brow at me as she hands me my drink.

"Well, if you want to watch Lydia play, then yes. If you're watching to see me coach, then no."

"You won't be coaching for them anymore?" Mom asks, jaw dropping in shock. "What happened?"

"I was having inappropriate relations with one of my players."

Mom's eyes flit to Lydia. "Assuming this has something to do with you?"

"Uhh…" Lydia looks to me.

Well, here goes nothing.

"I'm a lesbian, Mom, and Lydia and I are dating."

Her eyes dart between the two of us, waiting for more. "And?"

"And?" My jaw drops. "You're okay with this?"

Mom sips her drink. "Why wouldn't I be?"

"Well, Marcy's son—"

"Marcy's son? What does he have to do with this?"

I swig my drink. "He and his husband got divorced. You said it went against the institution of marriage."

"Because they were cheating on each other. They were trying to outdo one another. Didn't I tell you that?"

I shake my head. "I would have remembered that."

"One of them was having an affair so the other decided to go sleep with half the town to prove a point that he could do it too."

"Really?" Lydia asks. "Doesn't sound like they were compatible."

"And then they had a screaming match in the middle of the square during the farmers' market to air out their dirty laundry. It was quite the scandal." Mom clucks her tongue. "But that has nothing to do with you, dear."

I shove a hand through my hair. "I thought you were judging them because they were gay. And I thought you'd hate me because I like women."

"That's what you thought?"

Tears start to well in my eyes. "Yes. It made me anxious to tell you who I really was. I didn't want you to disown me."

"Oh, sweetheart." Mom pulls me in for a hug. "I am so sorry I made you think that I wouldn't accept you."

Tears start to soak my cheeks as I inhale her familiar floral perfume.

"Nothing you do could ever make me *not* love you. You, my sweet daughter, are the best person, and you would make any woman the happiest person in the world."

"Well, one makes me happy in particular."

"Well, it's nice to meet the woman my daughter is dating. I'm Vanessa." Mom still has one arm wrapped around me and extends her other hand for Lydia to shake.

Lydia takes it, but Mom pulls her in for a hug.

"Are we only dating?" Lydia goads. "It feels like more."

A watery laugh slips out. "That's what you're thinking about right now?"

"Don't get me wrong. I couldn't be happier that this went better than you thought, but at the same time, dating? Really, D?"

Mom laughs and it helps to break the tension inside of me.

"I have a feeling I'm going to like you, Lydia," Mom tells her. "Why don't I make us something to eat and we can get to know one another."

"That sounds good," I say.

Mom walks around the counter and Lydia takes her spot. When I started today, this isn't what I planned on doing.

Trying to save my job *and* my relationship? Yes. Although, I only managed to save one.

Now, having my mom pulling out a box of mac and cheese to start cooking with Lydia here? I never thought this is where I'd be.

"Are you okay?" Lydia whispers.

"It's weird she knows now."

"And you're okay with it? I mean, we did kind of spring this on her."

Looking up at Lydia, a sense of contentedness washes over me. "I mean, I wish I didn't have to lose my job to have all of this come out, but I can't say I'm not glad she knows."

"I'm glad Vanessa knows too." Lydia tucks a lock of hair behind my ear. "I don't want you to have to hide yourself from anyone. You're too wonderful a person to not show the world who you really are."

"I agree," Mom chimes in. "Which makes me love you even more already, Lydia. Delaney deserves someone who thinks the world of her."

"Don't worry." Lydia kisses me. "I do."

I pull her closer. It seems like both of us were trying to chase down these ideas of family, but it turns out, we already had everything we needed. I was holding on to something while hiding my real self. Lydia was holding on to the past. But together, we're creating our own version of family. The two of us together.

I might have lost out on the dream job, but I have my dream girl. The only one I've ever wanted.

What else do I need?

Epilogue

___

LYDIA - TWENTY-SEVEN MONTHS LATER

"This is getting way too close," Angie tells me.

"Tell me about it."

My eyes glance to the clock, watching the seconds tick down, as if in slow motion. The game is tied, 2-2. There's less than five minutes left, and whoever wins this game wins the Cup.

"Maybe next time they get here, you can tell them to make it a little easier on us," Troy says, nudging my shoulder.

"We can only hope."

Toronto's NHL team has been crushing it this season. I couldn't be more proud of Delaney and all her hard work with the Sixers.

With each win that got them closer to the finals, the time the two of us spent together became more limited.

It was hard with the Rosebuds in the playoffs, but it was worth it.

Because we came home with the Cup. And now, I want Delaney to bring one home.

I want her cup to match mine.

"Do you want me to take him?" Troy asks.

"No. It's the only reason I'm keeping it together." I hold my new nephew on my lap as he snoozes in my arms, despite the crowd noise.

While I was sad that my brother didn't make it further in the playoffs, Maverick helped to soften the blow for everyone. Glancing at the clock, my nerves ratchet up even higher.

Two minutes left. Almost every fan here in the arena is on their feet. It's a hard-fought game, the puck going back and forth between the teams with the goalies working hard to block numerous shots on goal.

"C'mon. C'mon," I whisper under my breath.

Florida's center grabs the puck and takes off down the ice.

"Fuck. C'mon. Stop him!" Troy shouts from next to me, standing.

My heart is in my throat as he is chased down the ice. "Oh my God."

The crowd erupts as the goalie blocks the shot off his stick toward one of the Sixers players. He doesn't hesitate, knowing the urgency as he moves down the ice.

"Here, let me take him." Angie takes Mav from my arms.

"Thanks."

I stand, trying to keep it together as the wingers pass the puck back and forth. Florida's defense is setting up, but with a quick flick of the Toronto player's stick, the puck is sailing over the goalie's shoulder and into the back of the net.

"Yes!"

If I thought it was loud when our goalie stopped the puck, it's nothing compared to now as the lamp lights and the horn sounds.

"Fuck yes!"

Troy and I are jumping up and down, high-fiving people in the crowd around us. The players are jumping on top of each other at one end of the ice as my gaze flits to my wife, standing on the bench. Delaney and the head coach look as calm as ever.

I cup my hands around my mouth and shout, "Let's go, Delaney!"

I don't know how she keeps her cool. I'd be a basket case. As the lines change and the guys head back to the bench, she's whispering things in their ears.

There's less than a minute left now. I wring my hands together, as Delaney's mom squeezes my shoulder from behind.

"She's got this. We've got this."

I glance back over my shoulder, giving her a worried smile.

The action moves toward Toronto's goal, and Florida pulls their goalie in favor of another player on the ice.

Players are swarming as they fire shot after shot at the goal.

"Keep it up. C'mon! You've got this!"

I'm shouting my encouragement, even though they can't hear me from up here. The entire crowd is cheering them on.

Twenty seconds left.

Nineteen.

Eighteen.

Florida fires a shot that is a little too close for comfort, but our goalie blocks it. "Thank God!"

I cover my face with my hands as they keep fighting and pushing.

With ten seconds left, the crowd starts counting down.

"Ten more seconds! Come on!" Vanessa yells from behind me. "Let's go, Sixers!"

"I think I'm going to be sick," I mutter into my hands. "Oh my God! C'mon!"

"Three, two, one!"

"Your Toronto Sixers are Stanley Cup Champions!"

The announcer's voice echoes through the arena. It's hard to hear him over the sounds of cheers. Tears are pouring down my face as the guys are jumping on top of one another on the ice.

My eyes find Delaney. She and the coach are hugging. When she pulls back, her eyes are wet as she shifts her gaze to where our suite is.

I know it's hard for her to see us up here, but I can feel her stare. My ears are ringing with the noise. Pride is bursting from me at watching my wife coach her team to a Stanley Cup victory.

"They did it!" Vanessa pulls me in for a hug as I try to control the tears.

After Delaney was fired from the Rosebuds, Troy, through the NHL grapevine, found out that Toronto was looking for a new assistant coach after failing to make the playoffs. With a little bit of luck, Delaney was able to secure the position.

Thank God. She didn't have to leave Toronto, and before my second season started with the Rosebuds, Biscuit and I moved in with her.

It hasn't always been easy with our schedules, but I wouldn't have it any other way.

It's not long before all of us are being ushered down to the ice for the Cup presentation and postgame cele-brations.

Watching as the Sixers are presented the Cup, my heart swells with pride. Delaney deserves every moment in the spotlight. She is one of the most incredible coaches, and everyone on this team respects the hell out of her.

As the players take their turn with the Cup, Delaney spots us and comes over to us.

"You did it!" I sweep her into my arms, peppering her face with kisses. "Could you have made it a bit easier on us?"

"You?" She laughs. "I don't know how I kept my cool."

"Because you're amazing, dear," her mom says, coming in for her own hug.

"Thanks, Mom."

Everyone is showering her with love and praise. It makes the tears start again. Watching her have her moment is unlike anything I've ever experienced.

"What?" She turns to me, eyes glistening with her own unshed tears. Happiness is radiating off of her.

"I love you."

"I can't believe we did it." She comes back to me, wrapping me in a hug.

"Couldn't be the only one in the family that hasn't won a Cup." Delaney drops a sweet kiss on my mouth.

"Technically, I have three now," Troy jokes from his spot next to me.

"Really, Troy?" Dad laughs.

"Hey, watch out. I'm coming for you," I tell him.

"You know, I really hope your kids aren't like this," Mom says.

"I'd take them having kids," Vanessa says.

Delaney groans, burrowing her head into my shoulder. "Can't they just let us enjoy the win for more than a minute?"

I toss my head back in laughter. "Then they wouldn't be them."

"I can't believe we won," Delaney confesses, so only I can hear her.

"I'm so proud of you. You're the best coach, and you deserve your moment in the spotlight."

She smiles down at me. "And now we have a matching set."

"There's that." I press a soft, easy kiss to her lips. I can't wait for the celebrations to continue later tonight. But not right now.

There will be time for that later.

Because Delaney and I have all the time in the world together.

And it's fucking perfect.

Bonus Scene

I t's late in the game, only five minutes to go. Minneapolis is pushing hard, but we're giving them everything we've got.

Because the trophy is on the line. It's game four in the finals and we're up 2-1 in the series. If we win, we'll bring home Toronto's very first championship in women's hockey.

I can't think about that right now.

No.

Swigging my water, I hear Coach Bailey call for a line change and I'm up and over the boards. Skylar sends the puck my way and I take off down the ice.

My stickhandling skills? Nothing less than perfect ever since Delaney pointed it out. I know she's up in the family suite, having gotten permission from the team to be here tonight since the men's team is also in the playoffs.

Minneapolis's goalie deflects my shot, but Skylar is there for the rebound. Their defender is there, but Skylar's faster as she sends the puck back to me. This time, I'm ready.

Cradling it in my stick, I fire it toward the goalie's stick side and it sails in with an inch to spare. The horn lights up and holy shit.

We're up 4-2 now.

"Yes!" Skylar wraps me in a hug. "Way to go, girl!"

"It's not over yet," I tell her, as we skate back to center ice for the puck drop.

They'll be gunning for us now as the crowd celebrates around us. I can feel their excitement. No one in the arena sits for the final two minutes as we skate hard to ward off Minneapolis's advances.

With a minute left, they pull their goalie in favor of an extra skater. They're sending goal after goal toward the net, but Parker is there, blocking every one of them.

She's been on fire tonight. Hell, she's been the MVP of the entire series with how well she's been playing.

Thirty seconds.

A stray shot sails into the net, bringing a whistle and a stop in play. Skating to the bench, I grab my water and take a few sips.

"Not much longer now. Keep fighting, everyone," Coach Bailey tells us. "We've trained for this. Defense, keep doing what you're doing. You're looking good. Just a little bit more to go."

I skate back onto the ice as Skylar readies herself to take the face-off. Winning it, she sends the puck back to me before I'm swarmed by Minneapolis.

I fire it off as the crowd starts counting down the remaining seconds. Every one of our women are there to block their shots on goal. Skylar gets a rebound and sends it flying down the ice. Before Minneapolis can intercept it, the final horn sounds.

Gloves and sticks are flying as every single person on the team piles on top of one another.

"We did it!" Skylar shouts, tears streaming down her face. "I can't believe we did it!"

"I can," I say, wrapping her in a hug.

Because we played like badasses all season. Our schedules aren't easy with breaks for international tournaments, but we made it work.

Long nights. Travel. Being away from family.

Getting to hoist that trophy here in a few minutes?

It will have all been worth it.

"Can you believe this?"

Parker skates over to us, helmet and gloves flying off behind her.

"All because of you!" I pull her into our hug. "We couldn't have done it without you."

Championship hats are passed around as a long, purple carpet—for the league's colors—is rolled onto the ice for the presentation of the trophy. The silver trophy, made up of two hockey sticks holding a cup with skate marks on the inside, gleams as it's brought out.

My ears are ringing with the cheers of the crowd as the team owner receives the cup and gives a short speech about how well the team has played to get to this moment.

Skylar, Parker, and I all stand together as the trophy is passed to Coach Bailey.

"Thank you, fans, for helping us bring the championship home!" she yells to more uproarious applause. "We couldn't have done this without you. And to this team and our coaches. You played hard and stuck together to win this as one. I'm so proud of each and every one of you. Take out one member of the team and we wouldn't be here right now. Thank you for dedicating yourselves to this team. I love each and every one of you and am proud to say we're champions!"

Tears gather in my eyes as she lifts the trophy over her head before kissing the shining silver metal.

"Where's our captain? Lydia?" she calls out and I skate over to her. "It's only right that you get this first."

"Hell yeah!" Skylar drops her arm and pushes me toward Coach Bailey.

"I want it next!" Parker shouts as I skate toward center ice.

"Great game tonight," Coach says, passing over the trophy.

As I lift the cup overhead, confetti rains down and the tears finally spill over. We've worked hard to get here.

I kiss it before doing a lap around the rink. Fans are pounding their fists against the glass. I pass the cup off to Parker, then everyone takes their turn on the ice with the cup.

I spot where Delaney is waiting with our families as they're finally allowed on the ice. She holds her arms wide open as I skate into them.

"You looked amazing out there," she tells me, squeezing me close.

I bury my face into her neck, not caring that the tears are flowing. "I couldn't have done it without you."

"Nah, that was all you." Delaney pulls back, cupping my cheeks and wiping away the tears. "Your stickhandling skills looked amazing."

I beam back at her. "Good thing I had a pretty decent coach."

"Damn right." She kisses me.

The best, sweetest kiss of my life.

"There will be plenty of time for that," Vanessa interrupts. "Let us congratulate her too."

I laugh, wiping the last stray tears away as she gives me a quick hug before my family moves in.

"Guess I'm not the only champion in the family now." Troy laughs, giving me a hug.

"You know I won a championship with the national team, right?" I tell him.

"Yeah, but now we've both won one in the professional league."

"And maybe I'll be beating you by this time next year."

"Ouch." He feigns hurt. "That was a low blow."

"That's enough, you two," Mom says, eyes wet with tears. "Tonight is all about Lydia."

"That's right." I laugh, hugging her.

"I'm so proud of you, sweetheart. That goal to seal the game? It'll be in the highlight reels, for sure."

"Thanks, Mom."

"Really, Lydia." Dad pulls me in for a hug. "I'm so proud of you."

"Thanks." I squeeze him close. "I can't believe we did it."

"It was a great series. You had me nervous there early on."

After a slow start, we pulled it together in the second period. I wouldn't have wanted to go back to Minneapolis to play the final game there.

"Thankfully we had the home crowd behind us."

"And now that means we get to celebrate," Delaney says, wrapping her arms around my shoulders.

I spin around and kiss her again. "There will be plenty of celebrations tonight."

"Mmm. I can't wait."

Right now, this moment couldn't get any better. Being in my wife's arms, surrounded by family, this is more than I ever could have hoped for when I signed with Toronto.

This team? Well, it gave me everything I ever wanted.

Want more of Lydia? Check out Best Kept Secret now. Or check out Changing The Play and how her parents meet.

Acknowledgments

BOOK TWENTY-NINE IS OUT IN THE WORLD!

How in the world is Love Pucked book TWENTY-NINE?! It seems like just yesterday I started writing, and this October is my 5-year writing anniversary. I absolutely love writing love stories, and getting to write a sapphic hockey SERIES?! I cannot wait to continue writing these ladies' stories

I have been so blessed to have so many amazing author friends that have been with me on this journey. I love you all so much! To Tina…one of my favorite people in the book world..I love you!

Thank you to my amazing beta reader, Delani (not quite my Delaney!), for making this book what it is! I adore you! Thank you to every person that has read, reviewed, shared, created edits, TikToked…you name it, your support has been the best part of this journey. To my Street Team and Influencer Team…your excitement for my books always puts a smile on my face! And my Facebook group…this place continues to be my favorite corner of the internet.

And to all the readers…I hope you love this new world and can't wait to dive back in like me!

<3 Emily

About the Author

After winning a Young Author's Award in second grade, Emily Silver was destined to be a writer. She loves writing inclusive stories, with strong heroines and the swoony men who fall for them.

A lover of all things romance, Emily started writing books set in her favorite places around the world. As an avid traveler, she's been to all seven continents and sailed around the globe.

When she's not writing, Emily can be found sipping cocktails on her porch, reading all the romance she can get her hands on and planning her next big adventure!

Find her on social media to stay up to date on all her adventures and upcoming releases!

Coaching in the women's hockey league is my dream. What I didn't plan on? Having to coach my ex...

When I took the job with the Toronto Rosebuds hockey team, I never thought I'd be reunited with the woman that ruined me for all others.

Lydia Bishop.

Playing hockey and Lydia are my past. My future is with this new team. Lydia is a distraction I can't afford.

The more time I spend with Lydia, the more I realize I might not be as over her as I thought. Until one night, we cross a line. *A line I don't want to come back from.*

She's my player. I can't be seen with her. Sneaking around is our only option until the world finds out about us and I'm forced to choose.

The future I've always wanted or the past I don't want to let go of.

I am so pucking screwed...

Love Pucked is a sapphic, second chance, hockey romance with a guaranteed HEA!

- -

EMILY SILVER

WWW.AUTHOREMILYSILVER.COM

LA TENTAZIONE DI LEVI
USA TODAY BESTSELLING AUTHOR
JULES BARNARD